DARKNESS

DARKNESS

RATNAKAR MATKARI

TRANSLATED FROM THE MARATHI BY
VIKRANT PANDE

HarperCollins *Publishers* India

First published in English in India by
HarperCollins *Publishers* in 2019
A-75, Sector 57, Noida, Uttar Pradesh 201301, India
www.harpercollins.co.in

2 4 6 8 10 9 7 5 3 1

P-ISBN: 978-93-5357-333-1
E-ISBN: 978-93-5357-334-8

Typeset in 11/15 Warnock Pro at
Manipal Technologies Limited, Manipal

Printed and bound at
Thomson Press (India) Ltd

This book is produced from independently certified FSC® paper to ensure responsible forest management.

CONTENTS

BIRTHDAY

14 November 1980

It would have been my Jeetu's ninth birthday.

We had celebrated eight of them – each like a festival, with family and friends coming together under our roof. But never again.

Jeetu is no more! He succumbed to meningitis on 14 October, but we knew of his impending death eleven months before that day. His mother did not believe it then, but I knew it was coming for him.

Knowing someone's date of death, before it arrives to claim them, does not soften the blow or the sorrow that follows in any manner. Tell me: how does a parent prepare for the death of their boy – their adorable, eight-year-old boy?

Eleven months ago, the very thought of his death seemed unreal, and even though I knew it was approaching, we would not stand for it to be spoken about out loud.

14 November 1979.

Jeetu's eighth birthday.

Also being Children's Day, we invited a few orphans from the local ashram, along with our friends and relatives. Around fifty orphans arrived at six in the evening, accompanied by an elderly gentleman. Most of them wore white half-sleeved shirts over clean, if slightly crumpled, khaki trousers. Much to my surprise, they had brought all the paraphernalia of a small music band.

'They never go to parties empty handed, you see,' their teacher explained. 'I tell them not to depend too much on charity, so here they are: ready to repay kindness with music.' Moved by the gesture I praised them to our guests, and the children were all smiles as they performed.

Soon, their musical performance gained momentum. The lights burnt bright, balloons floated about and the guests mingled without a care in the world. Dinner was served and everyone seemed happy. Jeetu, wearing a golden Jodhpuri suit, was busy receiving presents, with polite words of thanks, and touching the feet of the older guests in exchange for their blessings.

I noticed the children from the ashram mingling comfortably with the other boys and girls. It dawned on me that children did not understand divisions of class.

Within no time, the kids from Colaba, wearing imported and fancy t-shirts, were busy back-slapping the orphans as they laughed over jokes, unmindful of their clothes or where they came from.

I had this intense feeling of being watched. It was then that I noticed a pair of bright eyes following me: it was a boy sitting quietly in a corner. He had arrived with the orphans but was not wearing the khaki trousers. Instead, he wore a kurta–pyjama and looked much healthier than the other children, his dusky complexion especially radiant. It was his eyes which really attracted me to him in the first place. They seemed to be following me.

'Why are you sitting there all by yourself?'

'Huh?' he asked, as if snapping out of a reverie, and smiled. It was a strange yet endearing smile.

'Did you eat?'

'Yes,' he said, nodding his head. His smile *was* mesmerizing; so were his eyes.

'Come, let's go and meet others,' I said, nudging him to get up.

I introduced him to Jeetu. 'This is my son, Jeetu. It's his birthday party.'

At that moment, one of my Parsi friends, a wealth lady, walked over and kissed Jeetu on each cheek, much to his embarrassment. 'Many happy returns of the day, dikra! May you live long!' she said.

Jeetu immediately bent to touch her feet. 'You're going to cherish this present all your life, my boy!' she said, handing him a basket covered with a delicate shawl. 'After all, he's man's best friend.'

Jeetu pulled off the shawl in eager anticipation. 'A puppy! I always wanted a puppy, aunty! How did you know?'

'My Mariam had four pups two days back. Three were booked in advance. I was planning to keep the fourth, but then I remembered it was your birthday and figured you'd simply adore him!'

'He's so cute!' Jeetu said, unable to contain his excitement as he beamed at the little ball of fur sleeping in the basket.

'Only two-days old. Born on twelfth November, nineteen seventy-nine.'

'Twelfth November,' I repeated.

That was when it happened. The ominous thing that would change my life forever. In that moment of joy and cheer, the young orphan standing close beside me spoke: 'He will die on sixteenth November.'

'What?' I managed to ask after overcoming the initial shock.

'The pup will die on November sixteenth. The day after tomorrow,' the boy clarified, his voice firm with conviction.

'What did he say?' my friend asked, unable to understand his Marathi. I realized that telling her the truth would have landed the poor boy in trouble. She could have beaten him up or turned hysterical, creating a scene. I changed the subject, asking about Parvez's business and even feigned interest in her son's guitar lessons. As expected, she prattled on until I handed her a bowl of ice cream.

Meanwhile, Jeetu and his friends were chatting away with the boy. He repeated, when Jeetu asked him about the puppy's death: 'I told you. He's going to die on sixteenth November.'

'So all the pups will die on the sixteenth, will they?' A college student prodded.

'I don't know about the others, but this one will.'

The conviction in his voice sent a chill down my spine. A cold silence had settled among the children who had heard him say it.

Finally, another college student from the crowd asked: 'Can you predict anyone's death?'

'If I know their date of birth – yes.'

'Well, mine's the twentieth of December, nineteen fifty-seven.'

The boy went silent for a long moment, as if he was trying to recall something.

'January thirtieth, two thousand and twenty-eight,' he said, finally.

'Well, at least I've got plenty of time,' the college student said, evidently relieved.

Our accountant, Mr Gore, had been listening to the conversation attentively. 'Can he predict the future?' he asked.

'No, but if I know your date of birth, I can tell you the date of your death.'

'What a fraud! How could anyone know that? Anyway, why don't you tell me mine? I was born on seventeenth February, nineteen twenty-nine.'

The boy was lost in deep concentration for a few moments before he answered, 'March fifth, nineteen ninety-four.'

'My god! I've got to watch my health,' mumbled Gore, before disappearing into the crowd.

'I don't believe you,' a bespectacled college student said. 'June tenth, nineteen fifty-four.'

'Twelfth August, two thousand and fourteen,' the boy replied without so much as blinking.

The boy had become somewhat of a celebrity and a small crowd had gathered around him. They all acted like it was a little game. Clearly no one was taking the strange boy seriously, and if anyone did, they would have been reassured by the dates he gave them, which were all in the distant future.

It was a motley crowd, brought together by morbid fascination. There were college kids, young women, retired old men and housewives. Whether they believed him or not, their sense of relief was palpable when he answered with faraway dates.

There was something about the young boy's face that made it difficult for me to look away. Perhaps it was the way his expression changed when he was offered a date of birth. It was as if he was not really speaking to the person who had asked the question. He would merely mumble the date of death in a dispassionate tone, as if recalling numbers from memory.

What was going on in his head? He did not imply that everyone born on a certain date would die on the same day. It was as if the person asking somehow mattered as much as their date of birth. Maybe he needed the date of birth to be able to calculate their probable lifespan. But his face ... his face told a different story. This – whatever it was – had little to do with arithmetic. It wasn't simply multiplying four or six digit numbers in seconds.

I told myself it could just as well be a game he was playing – entertainment bordering on the macabre. Regardless, it had everyone's attention and I dismissed any further thoughts on that subject.

That was when I heard it: a wail, loud enough to carry over the din. It was my cousin, Anant, around forty years of age, sobbing like a child! People were trying to console him, saying it was just a game, a fun activity and not one to be taken seriously. He was muttering, 'I have young kids and a wife to look after. How can I afford to die so soon?'

'That boy told him he would die on twentieth November – just six days from now,' I heard a man in the crowd telling another person.

Someone managed to take Anant to the other room. I was upset at his behaviour. What a childish thing to do, sobbing away like that. He had ruined everyone's mood. The boy then disappeared into the crowd. Others dispersed, having lost interest in him.

I saw him again when the boys from the ashram were preparing to leave. While saying his goodbyes, his teacher said, 'He will come later, don't worry.' He knew I was looking for him. I imagined he was not the teacher's favourite, given the way the elderly gentleman had spoken about him.

It was not until later that I found that strange boy. My wife was beating him black and blue. 'What happened? Why are you beating that poor thing?' I shouted.

'Poor thing, my foot! Ask him what he said,' she demanded, pushing Jeetu towards me.

Between sobs, Jeetu managed to utter: 'He said ... he said ... I will live for another eleven months.'

The ground beneath me shook. It was one thing to laugh at the fate of the young pup or even my cousin Anant, for that matter. But Jeetu? It was unbearable. No, it was impossible!

'So, you said eleven months from now, did you?' I asked, trying to lighten the conversation. The boy merely nodded.

'Yes. October fourteenth, nineteen eighty.' I knew he was not joking. There was an immense solemnness in his tone.

My wife was shaken. It looked like she knew it was not a prank. Had he shouted or screamed, she may have had a chance to call him a liar. But there he was: offering his answer without batting an eyelid.

The mother and son were sobbing but, for a strange reason unbeknownst to myself, I was calm. Almost still. I was hoping against hope that the prediction would turn out to be false. But I knew that making an issue of it was meaningless.

My wife, in the meanwhile, had dragged the boy down the stairs and pushed him out of the door saying, 'Liar! You are a fraud, a mawali, a cheat! Don't you dare show your face here again, understand? Otherwise, I will have to call the police.'

Something told me she was being unreasonable. It was not fair to throw a young orphan boy out in such a manner.

But, somehow, I couldn't speak. I couldn't move.

16 November 1979.

The puppy was dead.

Jeetu was beside himself, wailing inconsolably.

They had grown attached to each other in such a short time. He had even bought a pram for Manek – that's what he had named him. Coloured balls, a bowl to sip milk; he had got so much for such a young pup.

The small, gentle creature that would lick Jeetu's palm and play about had grown weak and listless. Not eating and barely moving, Manek lay quietly in his pram. Jeetu's mother called for the vet, who, after examining the pup, shook his head in disbelief. He couldn't tell what was wrong. He flushed his stomach and gave him an injection. Nothing worked. The pup was dead by the evening.

We buried Manek in the garden.

Jeetu would not stop crying until, finally, we promised to get him a new pup, just like Manek.

For my wife and I, however, the poor animal's death marked the beginning of a nightmare.

When Jeetu was fast asleep, my wife finally said what was on our minds. 'It's true, isn't it? That … that boy predicted the dog's death?' Her voice was quivering.

'I don't know. Why do you ask?' I said, trying to dismiss her question.

'Yes, you do. You know. And if it's true, my … my Jeetu …' She broke into sobs and flung her arms over Jeetu, holding him close.

19 November 1979

I never mentioned the pup's death to Anant, but called his house regularly, on some pretext or other, and enquired about his health.

He always answered the phone. The paralyzing fear of death had kept him from stepping out of his house, and he had applied for leave until the twentieth. The poor man was paranoid, but at least his health seemed fine.

It was possible that the pup's death was a coincidence. It was possible that nothing bad would happen to Anant. Or to Jeetu.

21 November 1979

Yesterday, Anant died.

Though there was no rain or strong wind, one of the walls of his house collapsed. Within seconds, he was buried under a ton of bricks.

And that was it. Jeetu would not live much longer.

That bright-eyed boy had been battered for telling the truth.

And to think that my wife had dragged him out of the house! Pushed him out, shouting and screaming obscenities at him. Because he had spoken the truth. Just because we did not like what we had heard.

I felt like a criminal. I had to bring him home to apologize.

I felt a pang of guilt. It occurred to me that we could adopt him, bring him to a home where he would not be treated like an outcast for his abilities. It was the least I could do. Jeetu would only be with us for eleven more months, but that boy ... I needed to find that poor, bright-eyed boy.

I would treat him well. I would treat him like Jeetu, and he would become just like our Jeetu. Through him, our son would remain with us even after the eleven months were up. He was the answer.

Surely my wife wouldn't refuse. She would love the idea. This was the only way to keep our son. Our Jeetu! Our bright-eyed Jeetu.

22 November 1979

I went to the orphanage and met the elderly gentleman who had accompanied the kids the other day. He seemed happy to see me.

'What brings you here?' he asked as he served me tea.

'Well, I was wondering...'

'Please, don't hesitate, sir,' he said.

'I was looking to adopt a boy. He had come to Jeetu's party the other day and I figured, if he likes us and our home, he could join our family.'

The man brightened. 'What more could we ask for? I'm thrilled. Which of the boys did you have in mind?' he asked.

'He was wearing a kurta–pyjama … and he stayed back after you left with the others.'

The man frowned in concentration. 'Oh, that boy…'

'Is there a problem?'

'He's not one of ours. Sure, he visits and tags along on some trips but … I don't know much about him, frankly.'

'I see,' I said with a deep sigh. 'Well, when you meet him next please do send him to my house.'

'Of course, but … if you don't mind, could you consider adopting some other child,' the gentleman suggested.

I got up and left without any further comments.

23 November 1979

It happened last night. I was strolling in the garden after dinner. It was a starlit sky. I turned to see him standing there.

'I got your message,' he said.

'Message?'

'That you were searching for me?'

'Oh, well … it turns out you were right. The pup died. Anant died. And Jeetu will too … right?'

There was no surprise or remorse on his face. No sign of joy or relief at having been proven right.

'Tell me. It is true, isn't it? About Jeetu?'

'Yes. What about it? And why was Anant uncle so upset? The pup did not cry about it. Everyone dies.'

'Son, death is a grown-up fear. Once you grow attached to the world and all it has to offer, you will know why it's terrifying to think of leaving it all behind. Young minds are not as entangled in worldly matters. I suppose that makes it easy for young ones like you.'

He smiled.

'Will you live with us?' I asked. 'Here, in our house? We'll get you whatever you want. We will celebrate your birthday too, just like Jeetu's. When is your birthday?'

'Twelfth March.'

'Can you predict your own death?' I asked before I could stop myself.

'Yes, but it doesn't scare me.'

'What is it?'

'Fifth June, nineteen sixty-five.'

DARKNESS

'There are so many unsolved mysteries in the world,' the doctor said.

The police inspector merely smiled. The sarcasm was not lost on the doctor. He believed in what he had just said. He knew what he had experienced, but it was difficult to convince others. Especially those who did not believe in such things and spent their lives tracking down criminals and looking for evidence. For proof.

In the police officer's experience, once a criminal was caught, all questions could be answered and no mystery remained. There were many cases which remained 'unsolved' or 'unexplained,' but the cause was often a poorly conducted investigation or a very clever crook.

It wasn't difficult to see why they disagreed. The doctor was, after all, a psychiatrist concerned with understanding the mysteries of the mind. He believed that some facets of human behaviour were beyond explanation, leading only to a wall of impenetrable darkness.

He said, as he poured beer into a mug, 'Inspector, you too will experience it one day, I am sure. There are so many things in the world that cannot be explained, no matter how you look at them.'

'Let it be, doctor.' The inspector laughed. 'Your mad patients have corrupted your brain.' The inspector knew he had struck a nerve with the word 'mad'.

'My patients are not mad, they simply behave differently from others. There is a mystery or enigma behind their behaviour. Most often we are able to find a cause – that's our job – but once a while, we are unable to find answers.' The beer was taking its effect now.

A single lamp cast its light over their comfortable garden chairs and the table between them. The rest of the room was in darkness. The doctor felt as if the darkness was closing in on them. Of course, he knew it was his beer causing the sensation.

'Let me tell you about a recent case,' the doctor said. 'I haven't yet found an explanation for it and, trust me, it will leave you shocked.'

'Shoot,' the inspector said, lighting a cigarette as he sat back comfortably.

Event One

When the youth stepped into his office, the doctor was not sure of what to make of him. That was unusual.

He would, most often, get a good sense of the problem by just observing his patient – the way they walked in, their body language, their eyes. He would be able to make an assessment even before the patient spoke.

This youth looked quite normal and wore a tailored suit befitting an executive from a large, successful company. He walked in with an easy gait, almost as if he was a sales representative from a pharmaceutical company. In fact, the doctor only knew he was a patient because he had booked the appointment in advance.

'It's quite a strange story, to be frank,' he began. 'I'm not even sure if a doctor can help. Nothing is wrong with me. My health is fine, but the experience I have had is beyond any rational explanation. I realized it must be my imagination. I thought it best to talk to a psychiatrist.'

The doctor listened patiently. Very rarely did his patients exhibit such a clear understanding of their situation. He felt a hint of admiration towards the patient, who began narrating his story.

'These days, I feel very sleepy in the afternoons,' he began. 'Even though I sleep well at night, I just cannot keep my eyes open. I'm like someone who has taken a sleeping pill or is too drunk. I ask the guard outside my office not to allow anyone in and then, shutting the door, I put my head on the table and sleep. After an hour, I wake up fully refreshed and then get back to my work.'

'You're overworked. Your body needs rest and you should consult a physician,' the doctor said.

'There's more. Earlier I used to sleep without dreaming – like a log. I would have no idea of the time of the day, and there would be total darkness.

'But, over a period of time, I started seeing things through the darkness. I could see myself clearly, as if I were looking into the mirror. I'm not sure if that was a dream. When looking in the mirror one is aware of what one is seeing and there is a certainty of the way the image would behave. But, at that time, I was looking at myself like a third person observing two different individuals. Yet, the person I was looking at was me!'

'What were you doing when you realized you were looking at yourself?'

'I was ringing the doorbell of a flat,' the man said. 'After a few moments, the door opened.'

'And there was a beautiful lady standing there?' the doctor prompted.

'How did you know that?' he asked, surprised.

'Wishful thinking! Daydreaming. After all, a handsome man like you would have a beautiful girl in his dreams,' the doctor said, laughing.

The man looked at the doctor, who was also rather attractive for a man his age. In fact, he looked much younger while laughing.

'Maybe. There might be some truth in it,' he said, smiling. 'But let me tell you. I am married and my wife is no less attractive. She is modern and very affectionate. I can say my married life is the picture of happiness. We love each other dearly and I cannot even dream of being with some other woman. Well, that doesn't *seem* to be true ... but...'

'I have understood the situation,' the doctor said, nodding. 'Continue.'

The man hesitated. He seemed embarrassed to speak and wiped his forehead nervously. 'There is more "wishful thinking", as you say...'

'Go on.'

'I mean, the way a young man would feel when seeing a beautiful woman. She was alone. I hugged her at the door. Hand-in-hand we went to her richly decorated bedroom and threw ourselves on the soft bed.'

'And then you got intimate,' the doctor said, enjoying the conversation.

'Yes,' the man said. His blushing smile told the doctor that he had enjoyed the experience. 'But I didn't wake up when things got intense. I got up and had a glass of water before leaving the house. After that, there was darkness once more. As if I was drowning in deep water. I woke up to find myself in my office. An hour had passed.'

'What is there to worry about?' the doctor asked, still pulling his patient's leg. 'You were enjoying the company of a beautiful woman. It might have been in your dreams, but nevertheless, enjoyable. What's wrong with that?'

'I would have enjoyed it ... had it been just a dream,' the young man said. 'But it wasn't just a dream. There is some truth in it.'

'Yes. The emotions behind it are real.'

'Not just the emotions, doctor! There is something more to it. It feels like what happened was real, and that makes me uncomfortable. That's why I'm here. I feel like this uneasiness will drive me insane.'

'Why do you think it was real?'

'It's difficult to explain, but there are minor reasons. The flat, the bedroom and even the woman – they're so familiar. Like I've seen them somewhere.'

'There is a simple explanation for it. The flat is yours and so is the bedroom. In dreams, familiar things take on different shapes. That's what is happening here.'

'What about the woman? She is definitely not my wife. Her face is different. I am not able to exactly describe it. I am not able to see it clearly, but I can sense the beauty.'

'It is surely a dream,' the doctor said firmly. 'There is not an element of truth in it. Tell me – you go out of a closed office and then return. Will anyone believe it?'

'I don't mean that,' the man said, getting a little irritated. 'It is my mind that visits the place. I have read somewhere that if the mind can go anywhere in a particular form, even the body can take shape elsewhere.'

'That is the problem! You read something and then start believing in it,' the doctor said, rejecting his theory.

'I too would have believed it was a dream,' the young man said, 'but one thing is true: when I wake up, I know that I have had sex with her. That cannot be untrue.'

'Your case does need some more attention,' the doctor admitted. 'It is a strange combination of reality and dreams.

Let a few days go by. The situation may change. You may stop having these sensations.'

'No, doctor! This needs to stop as soon as possible, or it will end in disaster,' he said, getting upset. His self-control and calm demeanour were nowhere to be seen. 'I am in danger.'

'Danger? What kind?'

'I don't know. Maybe my life is at stake. I cannot pinpoint it, but I feel it. Whatever is happening is increasing day by day. Earlier our intimacy was limited, but now it has crossed all limits and I feel her husband is aware of it.'

'What?'

'Yes, her husband! He suspects something. She told me that.'

'How is that possible? There is no question of her husband. Just imagine that she is unmarried. She is alone.'

'I can, but that is not the reality. She is married and her husband now knows.'

'That is not true. It's a dream. You have created her husband in your mind. Describe him to me,' the doctor said, challenging him.

For a moment their eyes met. The young man seemed scared.

'I ... I have not seen him yet,' he said.

'And you won't see him because he does not exist.'

'He does! I'm scared of him. She is too. And the fear is consuming us both. Even in our most intimate moments we think he will come in and see us in that state and then ... he might not hesitate to do something in a fit of anger.

Something terrible is going to happen. I am sure it will. Sooner rather than later.'

'The explanation is simple,' the doctor said. 'You are very conscientious and loyal to your wife. You love her. You consider cheating on her a sin. The crime you are committing is pricking your conscience. It troubles you like a sword hanging by a thread. You have given this fear the shape of a man, one who is going to kill you.'

The doctor himself felt that his explanation, while quite appropriate, seemed very theoretical. There was much more to this than met the eye...

'No, doctor. Something terrible is going to happen to me one day. That day you will know that it was not just a dream. But by then, it will be too late.' He continued his passionate appeal, 'Do something, doctor! Save me from myself. I don't want to commit adultery. I don't want to have any relationship with his wife, but I can't help myself. And he won't understand. He will come and ... doctor, I can feel it – he is coming...'

The doctor observed the young man. Fear was writ large on his face, the way a child screams when he wakes up from a nightmare. The child, paralyzed with fear, does not recover for a long time. The fear is real.

For the man, it was not a dream. It was real fear.

'I managed to convince him,' the doctor said, refilling the inspector's glass, 'but it did not help much.'

'What happened?'

'I got a phone call from him today. He was delirious. He said, "Doctor, he came home when we were in bed. He rang the bell and we were taken by surprise. But, suddenly, things turned dark and I was saved. But I am sure it was he who rang the bell. I am sure he will enter the room tomorrow. He has reached the door, doctor! Do something! He is there, doctor! He has come!" The man sobbed as he spoke. I couldn't understand the rest as he was mumbling.'

'Interesting. Very interesting!' the inspector said. 'But what's so mysterious about your patient? He might have looked sober once but clearly he's plummeting into insanity. He is confused between reality and imagination. Add to it his fear ... This is a clear case of an unsound mind. One doesn't need a psychoanalyst to identify this. There is no mystery about it, doctor sahib!' The inspector seemed quite convinced.

'Agreed! That is what I told him. I gave him tonics for general improvement, told him to do some mental exercises. But something else happened which made me think that the events were truly mysterious. I realized it was not just his imagination. There is something more to it!'

'What happened?'

'Strange. Something very strange.'

Event Two

It must have been only a couple of days since the young man's visit when the doctor's phone rang. The receptionist said, over the intercom, 'Doctor, there is a lady on the line...'

'Lady? Is it the wife of the man who was here a few days ago?'

'Maybe, but she did not say anything about him. She did not refer to her husband having visited.'

The address confirmed that it was his wife. She was desperate and wanted to meet the doctor as soon as possible. It sounded like an emergency.

The doctor decided to visit her; he happened to have some work that side of town in the afternoon. He was eager to see the house where the couple lived. He wanted to compare the house with the young man's description of the flat from his dreams.

'Oh, you're here! I was waiting for you,' the woman said, overwhelmed.

She looked quite nervous, like her husband had been. Surprisingly, she did not speak about her husband's problem at all. There seemed to be a different problem.

'Every afternoon I feel terribly sleepy, doctor ... I don't know how to explain it. While I am asleep the doorbell rings and I open the door to find a handsome man standing there. I cannot see his face very clearly, but I know he is a stranger. He comes in and we ... doctor ... I do things with him that I should only do with my husband. When I wake up, the man is gone. Yet, I feel a strangely satisfied, physically. I feel like I have made a mistake, like I have committed a sin. The guilt pricks at my conscience.' She paused, clearly embarrassed. 'I know you will dismiss it as a mere dream, but that is not the case, doctor! There is something strangely real about it. I don't know what. But I don't want it. I want to be free of it. I'm scared that something terrible might happen.'

'Does your husband know about it?' the doctor asked.

Her reaction was surprisingly strong. She shuddered and nearly screamed, 'No, no! I cannot afford to let him know. That is what I'm worried about. If he comes to know, he will move heaven and earth. I'm worried he may do something terrible in a fit of rage. I'm sure he will catch us one day, and that day is nearing. I can feel him standing at the door. He will ring the bell one day and I will be forced to open the door. Do something, doctor!' she pleaded. 'I need to stop sinning. Before he enters the house. My fear has made my life hell.' She started sobbing.

The doctor gave her a tranquilizer. She calmed down after a while.The doctor surveyed the house. It wasn't as the young man had described. It was not as spacious or as richly decorated. It was quite ordinary.

The woman was quite calm by the time the doctor left. But now his mind was whirling.

The room was silent. The doctor had described the second event to the inspector. The lamp above swung slowly, throwing shadows on the table. Empty beer bottles lay upon it. Both the inspector and the doctor were in a trance, numbed by the effect of alcohol. There was no energy left to argue or debate. The inspector did not feel like probing or instigating the doctor further. They took each other's leave. There was a light drizzle. The inspector put on his overcoat and stepped out, eager to get to bed.

Even as the inspector lay in his bed, sleep eluded him. Both the stories were similar. The pattern was similar. He was sure he could solve the mystery. Was it a coincidence that both the husband and wife suffered from the same delusions? Or was there something else? How much of it was real and what part was imagination? He could not reach a conclusion.

He looked at the office door. It was shut. He looked around the room. He was back in his safe place. And, more importantly, he was alive!

He let out a deep sigh of relief.

'I may be alive today, but that does not mean I'll survive tomorrow,' he said to himself. 'I need to stop this. I must see the doctor...'

He needed to speak with someone and explain his situation.

He dialled the doctor's number but it was engaged. He waited impatiently for a few minutes and dialled again. The receptionist picked up the phone. 'The doctor has not come in yet,' she chirped. He left his number with her.

But he had to speak with someone. The matter was delicate. Who else could he trust?

He took a piece of paper and started writing a note for the doctor...

Event Three

He was standing in her bedroom.

She stood there holding two glasses of sherbet as music played softly.

He gulped down the sherbet and held her in a tight embrace.

He took a deep breath, inhaling the lovely fragrance of her hair. She gently moved away. He held her hand tightly and pulled her towards him.

A shriek escaped her lips. The glass fell down.

But the shattering of the glass did not make any noise thanks to the soft carpet.

There was no place for such noises. Everything was quiet, calm.

The next moment, they were in each other's arms and then in the bed.

They undressed and moved to the rhythm of the music, their bodies becoming one.

There was a sudden interruption. They both sat up with a jerk, moving away from each other.

There was someone at the door.

He put his hand to the doorbell, but it did not ring. Instead, it let out a high-pitched wail.

They both stood up, their screams frozen in their throats. Slowly, they opened the door.

He stood there like an enormous shadow. He stepped in, approached them. His shoes did not make a sound on the carpet.

Moving his hand to his pocket, he pulled out a revolver. And fired three shots.

His naked body collapsed on the bed, and his blood dripped on to the carpet below.

She screamed, but there was no sound. Overcome with fear, she collapsed on the bed and everything went dark.

He opened his eyes, surprised that he was still alive. He heaved a sigh of relief.

It was just a dream.

Dream? There was something real about it. But what exactly? He was confused. He went through the events in his mind. Yes, they were real...

But his death? That could not be real. There wasn't a scratch on him. Then the murder? Who was killed? Who did it?

The inspector was in his police station when he received the message. He sat there trying to solve the puzzle involving the lover, the woman, the husband. In one story he was the husband while in the other, the lover. The victim in one and the murderer in the other. *If we combine the two events...*

When the police entered the office, he was sitting at his desk – still overcome with relief.

'We are arresting you for a murder,' the officer said, taking him by surprise.

He had no idea of the dreams his wife had been having and was taken back to his house, where the murder had taken place there. The inspector looked more confused than the accused.

It was a murder. There was no doubt about it. One could guess who the murderer was, but there was no definite proof. The evidence was, in fact, adding to the confusion. Imagination and reality were intermingled.

The murderer was in his office when the murder took place in his own house. The woman stood numb with shock, unable to speak. There was no connection with the victim, and no telling why he was there. It was all confusing.

The inspector gave up and stared at the victim: the doctor. He lay riddled with bullets.

BY THE CLOCK

Mr Pundalik, a government auditor on official tour, was impressed with the local dak bungalow, where he had taken up residence. It was clean and he was well looked after, all thanks to the caretaker, Ramratan.

As Mr Pundalik was getting ready to leave for work, Ramratan entered the room. 'Mrs Pirojbai has invited you to dinner tonight,' he said.

'Pirojbai...? Do I know her?'

'She's the only living member of one of the oldest and wealthiest families in town. Must be seventy or so. Lives in a big mansion and everything. She always invites visitors over for dinner and drinks. In fact, she's even suggested you stay the night, since it will be too late for you to return.'

'This evening? Well, I don't have any plans. Tell her I'll be there. It's always nice, meeting new people.'

'Sahib...' Ramratan hesitated. 'May I suggest you don't stay there overnight...?'

'Why? I could use the change. And the company. Are you worried a seventy-year-old woman's going to eat me up?'

'Sahib, I know of two separate instances I should tell you about. Both involve men who stayed over at her mansion. Both were found dead within four or five days – heart attacks, they say.'

'If she had poisoned them, they would have died that very night. Anyway, get the car ready. I think I'm in for a pleasant evening.'

Ramratan lingered for a moment before nodding. 'Well, I did warn you...' he muttered as he left.

Around seven or eight years ago.

Pirojbai was all alone in her mansion, the servants having left for the day. Sleep eluded her, as it did on most nights, and it was well past midnight when she finally dozed off in her chair.

Suddenly, she was woken up by the sound of a clock striking the hour. She heard twelve dings. After a brief pause, the clock struck another five times.

There was no grandfather clock in her mansion.

Her blood ran cold and it was almost dawn before she fell asleep again. She had kept the light on the whole night. That was when it happened a second time. The clock struck twelve and after that, as she expected, five times more.

What's happening? Was it just her imagination? Or was it a warning, a threat, a premonition? Was it about … death?

The clock struck again just before sunrise. This time, Pirojbai was wide awake. Twelve … followed by five. She remembered a tale from her childhood in which the sound of a clock in such a fashion predicted the listener's death. The number of strikes after twelve told the number of days the listener had left.

I'm going to die in five days … Her mind raced to find a way to delay it. She invited Dr Rustomjee over for dinner and asked him to stay back and keep her company. She wanted to know if he could hear the clock too, but refrained from mentioning it. After all, she didn't want to seem like a senile old woman.

That night, Pirojbai expected the sound to wake her again. Meanwhile, Dr Rustomjee was asleep in a bedroom at the other end of the corridor.

At midnight, Pirojbai woke up to the sound of the clock. Twelve and then four. A day had been struck off and only four remained.

The next morning, when Pirojbai and Dr Rustomjee were having breakfast together, he said, as she served him coffee, 'I meant to tell you, Pirojbai, you are in the pink of health and should live for at least another decade.'

Pirojbai smiled. 'Tell me, doctor, how did you sleep last night? No disturbances, I hope?'

'Oh, don't ask,' Rustomjee began. 'I woke up three times to the sound of a damn clock striking *sixteen*. Please, scrap that old thing.'

That clock is why I invited you.

'Why do you keep that clock, anyway?' he asked.

'You won't believe me, doctor, but I haven't even found it yet. I turned the place upside-down, but it's nowhere to be seen.'

Dr Rustomjee left without saying a word, lost in thought.

Three days passed without a sound from the clock.

Three days spent wondering about her death. The fourth was unbearable, until finally, she got the news.

Radhabai arrived at night. She told Pirojbai that Dr Rustomjee had died of a sudden heart attack.

Pirojbai wondered what it meant.

Then she realized it. Rustomjee had heard the clock, a sound – a message – that was meant for her ears only. And so, her fate had befallen the poor doctor. She had redirected her death.

Over the course of the next seven or eight years, Pirojbai heard the clock many times. It indicated that she had five or six days left and, each time, she invited someone to spend the night at her mansion. It was a motley mix: a rich local businessman, a visiting history professor, a government servant who was staying at the local dak bungalow on tour, a police officer and, once, a lost traveller seeking shelter for the night. All of them heard the clock strike ... and they all died after five or six days of their stay. Each time the cause of death was a sudden, unexplained heart attack.

Now the striking clock was not a warning – only a reminder for her to find a substitute.

This time, she had found a certain Mr Pundalik. He had agreed to dine with her and then stay the night. She sat waiting for him, worried he would decline.

Mr Pundalik arrived, as promised, much to her surprise and relief. They enjoyed their drinks and conversation. It was a lovely feast with a large spread of chicken and mutton dishes. Finally, Mr Pundalik was shown to his room before she retired to her own.

Four days after Mr Pundalik's stay at the mansion, Radhabai came running to the dak bungalow. It was well past midnight.

She said, almost breathless, 'Ramratan, come with me to the mansion. I stayed back at the mansion tonight and was woken up at midnight by madam's screams. She was on the floor, clutching at her chest. It looks like she had a heart attack. Please come with me to get the doctor.'

Ramratan rushed to Mr Pundalik's room. He banged on the door to find it open. He hurried in and nudged Pundalik's shoulder saying, 'Sahib! Sahib, wake up! Mrs Pirojbai ... she had a heart attack ... we need the car to take her to the hospital.'

Mr Pundalik woke up, shielding his eyes from the bright light. He said calmly, as he reached for the dressing table near his bed, 'Wait, Ramratan. Let me get my hearing aid. You know I am stone deaf and never sleep with them on.'

After plugging them in and arranging his hair over them, he asked, 'Now, tell me. What's this all about?'

THE HEIR

At times, life seems meaningless.

We each have our own theories and understanding of life. We define success differently and explain our failures based on our backgrounds, opportunities, wealth and whatnot.

Regardless of what that understanding or belief is, all it takes to shatter it is a small, almost avoidable event. After that, life and what we thought we knew about it, is forever changed.

You are left desperate and saddened, dismayed and without any options. A deep sense of disquiet fills your mind forever!

The event itself could be less than ordinary. You're like a child who kicks an unassuming ball only to discover it was a bomb. Just like that, you are left scarred for life.

What is this event? For me, it was accompanying Shankar to his village. That is all it was.

Shankar is a couple of years younger than me, and he's more than a friend – almost family, in fact. His father, Ramdada, was my father's close friend.

My father, a lawyer, committed suicide after I was born. Mother told me that a client had cheated him and he couldn't bear the shock. I never broached the topic again, seeing the way my mother had reacted when I had asked her.

He had been the only earning member, and after his death, my mother was left with an infant and no money. It was Shankar's father who came to our rescue. My mother earned a little, but it was thanks to Ramdada's largesse that we could run our household and that I was able to complete my education. Where does one find such people these days?

Unfortunately, Ramdada died before Shankar, his only child, could get a job. But he had left enough for the family. We were, in a sense, their dependents though we did not stay in their house. But Shankar never treated me as an outsider. Our friendship only grew stronger with time.

One night, Shankar came over and said, 'Shyam, we need to leave for Ranvali tomorrow morning.'

'Ranvali? Why?' I asked.

I had heard him talk about Ranvali before. It was their ancestral village. But he had never visited it. They had a large mansion there, which his uncle, his father's brother, looked after, supervising the domestic help.

'You know my uncle – the one staying at the mansion at Ranvali? He died a couple of weeks ago.' Shankar put it matter-of-factly; he barely knew the man.

'I got a letter from a lawyer,' he continued. 'My father was the only other family member. And now, I'm the only heir to the mansion. The lawyer wants to discuss the details.'

'Now, isn't that something...' I was genuinely stunned by this sudden stroke of luck. 'Here, in Mumbai, a two-room house is a big deal, but a mansion? Oh, Lady Luck's smiled at you.'

Shankar laughed. 'Can we go tomorrow?' he pleaded. 'That lawyer needs me there to go over some formalities. Might be a good idea to see the place and arrange for a caretaker. I need you to be with me.'

I was more than happy to accompany him. I was curious to see this huge mansion, which was going to be Shankar's now. It would be a picnic of sorts, a fun trip to his ancestral village.

The most frightful things begin in a beguiling manner. We believe we know where we are supposed to go, but it's destiny that decides our destination.

My mother, to my surprise, was a little reluctant to let me go with him, but Shankar was persuasive as usual.

I always told Mother about my plans, even if Shankar teased me about it. After all, she had sacrificed so much to give me her full attention when I was growing up. She had been a young widow and could have remarried, but raising me had been her top priority.

We boarded the bus to Ranvali the next morning. It was a long journey, and by the time we disembarked at the Ranvali village stop, the sun was at the western horizon. An elderly gentleman stepped forward and said, 'You must be Shankar.'

We were the only ones at that stop.

It was the lawyer. He was not a loquacious character, and without much of a preamble, we began walking towards the mansion. There were no porters or rickshaws. Luckily we were travelling light, with just a backpack each.

We walked along a wooded path, crossing small gurgling streams on the way. It was picturesque and the only sounds were the chirping of crickets and the occasional snapping of twigs under our feet.

No one spoke. For us, this was a different world, new and strange after years spent in Mumbai. The lawyer had switched on his torch to guide us. By the time we reached the mansion, it was almost nightfall.

The mansion, silhouetted in the moonlight, was an impressive sight.

'Shivrama!' the lawyer shouted.

Soon, an old man, bent with age, came running with a lantern in his hand. He must be the caretaker, I surmised. He had been expecting us and had prepared the dining room for our visit. Hungry, we wolfed down the food before he led us upstairs and showed us to our rooms. The lawyer shuffled his feet nervously. He said, clearing his throat, 'Shankar Rao, I would like to say something. I hope you don't misunderstand me.'

'Please,' Shankar said, waving his hand casually, as he lit a cigarette.

'The last occupant of this mansion was your uncle. You are the legal heir to the property, but as per your uncle's wish, and his will, you have to fulfil one condition.'

He was silent for a while. We both waited expectantly for him to continue.

'I know you are Shankar. You are carrying my letter as additional proof – not that I need any evidence. But the fact that you are the true heir will be known to me tomorrow morning.'

He went on, noticing the confusion on our faces, 'This mansion is quite safe, you know.' He looked around nervously and lowered his voice before continuing, 'It is more than three hundred years old. And there is something here that only the true heir to the mansion is able to see.'

What was he saying? We decided to remain silent and let him continue.

He repeated, wiping his forehead with his handkerchief, 'Only the true owner of the mansion will be able to see something here that no one else can.'

Shankar stood up. He said, 'I have no reason to stay here any longer. I don't want to be seeing ghosts in this damn place.'

'Wait! Shankar Rao, please don't get upset,' the lawyer pleaded. 'You are the true heir and the owner of the mansion. Please, believe me when I say no harm will come to you. The mansion loves its owner and would never hurt him. All you have to do is witness whatever you are meant to. Tell me the same the next morning. When I hear you, I will be convinced that you are Ramdada's only son. I will hand over the property papers to you.'

Shankar sighed resignedly. 'If you so insist, I will stay back. Why should I be afraid? I've got my friend with me for company, in any case.' He laughed nervously, trying to make light of the situation.

'Your friend is most welcome to stay with you,' the lawyer said, nodding his head. 'But let me make this clear: only the true heir will see whatever he is meant to. Your friend here won't be of much help.'

I am an atheist of sorts. The only person I blindly trusted was my mother. I hardly believe in gods, and wasn't about to let a ghost story scare me away. The old lawyer sensed my scepticism and said, 'This has been happening for generations here. It is not a joke, sir. I will be able to explain everything tomorrow morning when Shankar Rao tells us what he saw in the night. I will take your leave now. Best of luck!'

Shankar was a little disappointed that the caretaker had arranged for us to sleep in two separate rooms. We had hoped Shivrama would stay back, he but left soon after ensuring we were comfortable. He never spent the night in the mansion. Instead, he had a small hut on the grounds nearby, where he resided with his family. Asking him to stay back would have exposed our fears, so we watched him silently disappear into the darkness.

The moment he left, Shankar and I moved a bed so we could share a room. We had no plans of staying alone.

I took out a bottle of brandy and said, as I took a swig, 'Come on, now! This will help soothe your nerves. You look like you've seen a ghost!' I realized a tad too late that the joke was in poor taste. He glared at me while I laughed, slapping my thigh with my palm. He asked, as he took a long swig, 'Shyam, what if I don't see anything tonight?'

'You won't see anything, I am sure. I don't believe in such hocus-pocus.'

'But I need to see something, don't I? That lawyer's going to ask me. What do I tell him then?'

'Don't lose sleep over it, okay? We'll figure something out tomorrow,' I assured him. Soon, we were both tipsy, and eventually, dozed off. The lamp burnt itself out in the middle of the night.

A streak of sunlight from the ventilator woke me up. Shankar lay on the other bed, snoring peacefully. I could hear Shivrama in the kitchen downstairs.

I nudged Shankar, who woke up rubbing his eyes and said, 'Wow! I really slept well.' He said, after a pause, 'But nothing happened!'

'Didn't I tell you so? You were worried about nothing.'

'But what about our lawyer friend? He'll be asking me questions for which I have no answers now. If I don't answer to his satisfaction, he won't hand over the papers to me. These people are a superstitious lot, you know!'

I explained to him in detail what he should tell the lawyer. Now, it was up to him to make it dramatic and narrate it as if he had experienced it himself.

The lawyer arrived after we had finished our breakfast. He asked, as he sipped his tea, 'So, how was your night?'

Shankar was silent. He threw a nervous glance at me. I nodded encouragingly for him to continue. I said, to buy some time, 'Shall we go upstairs?'

The lawyer was a nervous man. He asked, as he kept his tea cup on a table, 'You did see something, didn't you?

'Let him explain,' I replied. I glared at Shankar to begin as we reached the room upstairs.

Shankar said, putting on an act which impressed me, 'A woman ... holding a baby. It scared me.'

'Please, Shankar Rao, go on!' the lawyer said, his voice gentle and encouraging.

'Go on, Shankar!' I added, hoping he wasn't about to chicken out.

'I was in a deep sleep when, at midnight...' he paused for dramatic effect and continued, '... the lamp went out. It was pitch dark. There was a soft light outside the door. It opened gently, without a sound. I could feel a soft breeze on my face. I was scared but somehow couldn't wake Shyam – he was snoring without a care in the world. So, I got out of bed and walked to the door ... as if in a trance. I was being pulled by some unknown force. The cool breeze was like a soothing caress.

'I found myself walking down the steps to the drawing room. That was when the clock struck twelve. And when the sound died down, I could hear soft ... sobbing. I looked around, but I couldn't see anyone. The weeping ... it got louder, and was joined by an infant's cries. I heard a man's angry outburst, but couldn't make out the words. The noise, the words, the sounds – they merged, reaching a crescendo. I tried squinting into the darkness but couldn't see a thing. All of a sudden, the room was plunged into a deep silence. I came back to my senses and walked towards the stairs when ... when—'

'When?' the lawyer prodded, eager to hear the rest.

'Then I saw it ... in a traditional nine-yard sari, rushing down the stairs. It was a woman's body. It was – she was ... headless. A headless body with an infant in her arms. Behind her, running after her with a cruel, cruel face was ... a large man with a sword. The woman screamed and then, in a flash, they were gone. Vanished.'

The lawyer wiped his forehead nervously as he glanced at Shankar, waiting for him to continue. And he did. 'I walked back upstairs and there, standing at my bedroom door: the headless woman with ... with these pieces of ... I couldn't tell at first. It could have been watermelon but ... it was all that was left of her baby. Just these raw pieces of flesh streaming blood down her arms.

'I must have fainted at the sight of it all, but I woke up in my bed.'

'Shocking. Absolutely shocking. But it's true,' the lawyer exclaimed.

'Shankar Rao, I had no doubt you were – *are* – the true and legal heir to this property, but it was my duty to fulfil the conditions laid down by your late uncle. Your uncle had seen something very similar.

'Long ago, a lady from your family had an affair with one of the servants in the mansion and gave birth to a child. Her husband found out and killed them. Since that day, the three haunt this mansion. But only the heir and owner ever sees them.'

The lawyer hugged Shankar, more out of relief than affection. He was a diligent man and was relieved that he had done his duty. He left hurriedly to finish his paperwork.

Shankar was still reeling from the shock when I said, 'What are you staring at? All ghost stories have a common theme!'

He said, visibly relieved, 'These superstitious old men! So easy to fool.'

His laughter echoed in the hall.

That was the day I lost my smile.

I was left with something I would never be able to share with anyone. Definitely not with Shankar. Yes, I had told him this little story. But it wasn't fiction. I had experienced every detail.

I had seen the three ghosts. And it was then that I knew I was Ramdada's eldest son, and Shankar was my younger brother. I was the true heir to the mansion.

All these years I had all but worshipped my mother, believing her to be a saint. But her affair with Ramdada ... Fortunately, my father hadn't harmed us.

The story of my past, my mother and father's, haunts me like an ancient ghost re-enacting a tragedy within the walls of a mansion. Nothing will ever be the same.

LADY OF THE HOUSE

Makrand came to meet me one morning and said, 'I came to repay the balance amount.'

I asked, smiling, 'So, you've finally decided to buy the house.'

'Of course!' Makrand said. 'You scared the hell out of me! But enough is enough. How could you pull my leg like that? I had so many sleepless nights.'

'Are you saying you never saw anything?'

'Let's not start that again, okay? That house is just fine and there is nothing of the sort you described. You almost cost me this beautiful house, trying to scare me off like that.'

I was amazed. What I had told Makrand was absolutely true – no exaggeration. On the contrary, I stood to lose at least a few thousand bucks by warning him off. But I had done my bit by cautioning him so at least my conscience was clear. I knew what he was in for, and I had been honest. Sure, I had taken a token advance and asked him to stay for a few months before he made the final payment. If he decided not to, I had promised to return the sum. Certain he would be back for his money, I had it ready. I wasn't just the seller after all – I was also his friend.

Unfortunately Makrand thought I was a liar. He said, 'I'm not saying you didn't experience what you say you did, but I believe these are signs of a weak mind. To tell you the truth, I've never had a better time in my life.'

'Really?'

Makrand smiled bashfully and added, 'It's been a month since I got married. She's really nice.'

'Married? You never told me!' I blurted out, a little angrily.

'We decided to have a private ceremony. Secondly, you were not in town then. Anyway, now take this money and let's close the deal. My wife's eager to see the house transferred in our name. Besides, I'm in love with the place,' he said, pushing the bundle of notes into my hand.

I was taken aback by his enthusiasm, but was a little relieved that he had had a good stay. Makrand then insisted I visit his new home and meet his wife.

I agreed. I wanted to see what Makrand would do with the place. It was also an opportunity for me to wipe out the sad image I had of it in my mind. Not that I could have refused, what with his childlike insistence.

The house had been transformed. The architecture was exquisite, no doubt, but I remembered it having an air of melancholy that sat against its broken edges and discoloured plastering. It used to look like a handsome man withering away with the ravages of a serious illness.

Now the house was almost unrecognizable with freshly painted walls, bright curtains and festoons at the door. The garden looked well maintained, and the rooms, neat and clean. The drawing room was furnished tastefully with various knick-knacks at selected corners. For a moment, I felt at a loss. What was it that Makrand had managed to find which had eluded me? A chill ran down my spine.

Makrand excused himself for a moment before returning to talk about how lovely the house was. After a while, the appetizing aroma of fried food wafted into the room.

Makrand continued praising the place and his wife, and soon everything in general. All the while, the memories gnawed at me. I couldn't forget the time I'd spent here: the deathly silence, the strange events and, of course, her.

She and her unearthly beauty.

I was overcome by fear and anxiety. I couldn't explain what was happening to me, but it was almost suffocating.

It had been love at first sight, the day I had stepped into the house. I had always dreamed of a beautiful sanctuary away from the chaos of the city. This was the place where I could spend my time away from my work, reading and relaxing. The owner had just moved away to Africa, selling me the house at a throwaway price. He seemed disinterested in the deal. I noticed his sad smile and his struggle to make conversation with me. But I did not know him well enough to ask about his personal life. Not that he opened up. I figured he was a private person, even though his grief was evident in his deep sighs, his intermittent silences and his faraway eyes.

It was clear that the man was desperate to sell the place, even though it hurt him to part with it. This was interesting, at the time, because it wasn't a very old house. I was left with many unanswered questions. I could make out that there was a deep connection of his sorrow with the house itself

My excitement over a big, new home was short-lived. Contrary to my earlier excitement of having purchased a neat bungalow for myself, as I entered the house a strangely gloomy thought enveloped me. It must have been my loneliness, I presumed. I expected quiet solitude, but stepped into an empty space that resounded with a deathly silence.

The nights in the house were cold, and the wind scraped a branch of the plumeria tree against the wall, each swipe like a gasp for air – just one of the sounds that played on my mind as I watched the moon from my bedside window. A multitude of thoughts crowded my mind. What seems ordinary in the day becomes melodramatic and exaggerated at night. My ears strained to hear any unnatural sounds but all I could hear was the whistling of the wind and the grating sound of the tree branch. I closed it and fell asleep, only to wake with a start.

A face stared at me through the glass pane. It took me a while to realize that I was not dreaming, but before I could get up, it vanished. The palms were the last to fade.

I stood up in a cold sweat. Switching on the light, I turned to the wall clock – it was half past three. A bright morning woke me up. The room was filled with cheery sunlight as sparrows chirped noisily in the garden. Dismissing my experience of the previous night from my mind, I got up enthusiastically.

Later that morning, I lit a cigarette and left the house, looking for a tea stall. I had arranged for a maid to come in at eleven, and had some time to myself until then.

I returned at half past ten, freshened up by a brisk walk in the cool morning air. I settled in a chair facing my bedroom, with my cigarette and a book.

When I looked up, my blood ran cold.

My bed – it had been made for the day, the blanket folded and the pillow in its place. I was sure I had left it unmade. And now, I was sure I had company. I was not alone.

I then noticed other details that made my hair stand on end. I found my clothes – which I had lazily tossed on the chair – folded neatly in the cupboard. The books had been arranged on the writing table. Was my mind playing tricks on me? I clearly remembered having stepped out of the house with all my things lying scattered as they had been the previous night. I wasn't a very organized person. But who could have come in? The house was locked and the windows were shut. The maid was yet to arrive. It could not have been a thief, for not a single thing was missing.

I then remembered the face at the window last night. A chill ran through me again.

Footsteps from behind made me turn with a start. It was the maid. She must have been taken aback, seeing me deathly pale at the sight of her. I asked, trying to hide my embarrassment, 'Do you have a key to this house?'

She glared at me for my accusatory tone. 'No,' she snapped.

The strange happenings continued. I had an old swing removed from the veranda, only to find it back in its place. I asked the maid about it that evening. 'Did you put that back?'

All she did was stare at me, which was answer enough.

'Look,' I tried to explain, 'this has been happening for the past few days. The bed gets made, things go back to their places ... I don't want to scare you, but do you think anyone else comes in here?'

Her face turned pale and she stared at me for a long, uncomfortable moment. She then left without saying a word.

She did not come to work the next day.

I was left alone with the mystery until, one day, I found the answer. And that left me with another problem.

It was around midnight. I put my book on the bedside table and switched off the light. I had nearly dozed off when

I heard a strange sound near the window. My ears strained. It was like water falling gently. After a while I realized that it was the gentle rocking sound of the swing in the veranda.

I sat up with a start.

I gathered whatever courage I could find and put on my slippers. I crept out of my room and the noise from the swing got clearer.

Finally, I managed to push open the door to the veranda. The creaking sounded loud in the silence of the night. The swing was empty but continued to move slowly. It stopped after a while. Whoever was occupying it had left.

I wiped the sweat off my forehead, feeling suddenly weak in my knees. I closed the door and returned to my room.

And there it was – a white apparition. It was gently caressing the wall near the table, as if it were a living being. It turned at the sound of my footsteps and the face took my breath away. It was a young woman, beautiful yet deeply sad. Within seconds, she started fading and soon she was gone. Vanished. A strange feeling came over me and I heard myself shout: 'Wait!'

The image appeared once again. I said, 'Wait! Don't go away. I want to talk to you.'

Her image sharpened further as I asked, 'Who are you?'

I wasn't sure if she would answer my question, but was amazed at my courage and presence of mind. I was no longer afraid.

Soon, she appeared in her full form. The glow had faded to reveal a pale face. I asked again, 'Who are you?'

Her lips spread in a weak smile. 'A woman. Or at least that's what I was ... when I was alive.'

'You are a ... a ...' The word 'ghost' was difficult to say.

She smiled again. 'Scared?'

'No. But ... what are you doing here?'

Her smile vanished as she replied, 'That's what I should be asking you.' There was a note of anger in her voice.

'I own this place.'

'Wrong. It is mine.' She spoke with conviction.

'You mean, you've been haunting it,' I said, my voice laced with contempt.

'Do you even know what you are saying? The dead may only return to a place that rightfully belongs to them,' she said firmly.

'And how is this your property?'

'My father built this house – for me.' She continued, 'I had plans for it. A beautiful garden. A decorated doorway. I had thought of paintings for these very walls. But before I could even begin, I lost my life in an accident.' She brushed her hair away from her neck as she turned her head for a moment.

I could see a dark scar, a mark, possibly, from the injury that had killed her. The blueish-black scar against the contrast of her fair skin looked dreadful. A shiver ran down my spine as I tried to imagine her horrible death.

'I could not fulfil my dream of making this place my home. And now I return to these walls, these hallways,' she said, her voice filled with anguish.

'But you would have left this place after you got married...'

'I had no such plans. I was an only child. I would have asked my husband to stay here.' Her eyes were gleaming now. I thought of the previous owner, forced to leave under the weight of this woman's sorrow. The thought of her wanting to take charge was discomforting. I had to find a way to remove her. I asked, 'Is there anyone else here, apart from you?'

'I would not stand for it. This is my home.'

Before I could react, she was gone.

Days went slowly by and I wondered why the woman, who longed for the place in death as much as she had in life, did not attempt to harm me – an interloper impinging on her solitude. One day, I even asked her why she hadn't tried to scare me away.

Smiling in her usual joyless way, she said, 'Ghosts are not monsters. Death does not change who we were, only how we exist.'

She looked human enough. In fact, she must have been a warm and kind person. I was reminded of a small and beautiful flower. All she wanted was for me to acknowledge that this house was rightfully hers.

I refused to do that.

It dawned on me that I might have been losing my mind, seeking out the company of a ghost. How long could it go on before my secret slipped through my own lips? I had to put an end to our conversations. But how?

It seemed cruel to ask her to stay away from the house, but I had no choice. There was no way I would agree to running or furnishing the place as she instructed, even though I had started doing things I thought would please her. But winning the favour of a living being was one thing…

I was jolted from my reverie when she put her hand on my shoulder.

'Did I frighten you?' she asked.

'Your hands … they're so warm!'

'Could you forget, for a moment, that I am not alive?'

'That's impossible. Can you?'

'I do look like a living woman, don't I? These days, I am able to retain my form for quite a long time. With practise I can improve, and after a while, I can be like this for days on end. Of course, I would have to return to formlessness now and again.'

'I can understand the form but what about the warmth? How do you…'

'My desire burns strong. How could I be cold to the touch?' She smiled and continued, 'To tell you the truth, it is not real. It is something only you feel. It is because I can influence your thoughts. You might even believe that I am alive and breathing.'

I was stunned. To think my mind was in another's control – it was an outrage.

'Get out.' I brushed her hand off my shoulder. 'Get out of here! I won't tolerate you any longer. Go now!'

Her sorrow was palpable. She looked surprised and shaken before she faded away.

That night, I woke up to the sound of her sobs at the window. They continued into the early hours of the morning. The sound made the air heavy.

There was a storm the next day.

I shut the doors and windows and remained in my room. Soon a power outage left the house dark. I lit a lantern and its flame danced against a cold draft, swaying the shadows. I remembered the sound of her weeping. I was terrified. Strange thoughts passed through my mind as I sat on my bed, watching the shadows move.

A loud bang.

The door was thrown open and the cold wind rushed in. I knew she had entered the room. I ran and bolted the door as she laughed.

'These things don't amuse me any more,' she said.

She had manifested in full, but in the light of the lantern I could see through her pale form.

Coming close, almost touching me, she said, 'You know how much I cried last night?' There was something childlike about the complaint.

I remained silent.

'Don't you feel anything for me?'

'I do. Trust me,' I said. 'But we can't be together. I want to keep my house, and you have to give this place up.'

'You want me to be gone forever?'

'The dead shouldn't return.'

'It's not that simple,' she said, with downcast eyes. The storm raged outside. After a while, she looked up at me.

'Why don't you want to be with me?'

'You know the reason.'

'I can behave like a living woman. You have seen that, haven't you?' She continued, as she put her arms around my neck, 'And you want me to disappear forever?' I could see her eyes looking into mine, searching for a glimmer of hope. I was scared, worried I would lose myself. 'I could be the doting wife and we would both own this house.'

'Enough!' I shouted, pushing her hands off me. 'What about me?'

She smiled, fuelling my anger, and said, a little mischievously, 'Why would a bachelor like you object to someone like me being available all the time?'

I was taken aback. 'Are you falling in love with me?'

She stared at the darkness outside the window for a long moment before she spoke again. 'The dead know only the love they felt in life – nothing more. I loved this house, which is why I still do and always will. But I can never fall in love.'

The lantern had burnt itself out and the room was filled with darkness. We sat silently for a while. Her eyes shone like fireflies.

I said, adding a tone of finality to my voice, 'I want you to leave this place.'

'I don't believe that,' she said as she faded away, her laughter echoing in her wake. There was bitterness and sorrow in that sound.

I woke up the next night to the sound of laughter. It was very soft, almost muffled. I ignored it and turned to face the wall.

That was when I noticed it.

There were no flames, but the wall was burning. Embers fell from the roof. I stared at the strange sight – a molten substance was flowing towards my bed.

Rushing to the bathroom, I picked up a bucket of water and tried to douse it. In an instant, it died out.

It was her ploy to scare me.

I woke up to a clear and beautiful morning. The previous night seemed like a distant dream as I went about my day. I felt invigorated by my determination to remain unfazed by the dead woman, but the feeling was shattered by what I saw.

There was smoke coming out of my bedroom.

I rushed to open the door. Flames consumed my bed and climbed up the curtains.

I managed to extinguish the fire with great difficulty but the event left me shaken. There was no doubt it was her doing, but the sight of a partially burnt down bedroom left me depressed. There were half-burnt clothes, a wet floor, and black patches on the wall.

This was not just anger, it was a reckless, childish tantrum. She must have been deeply hurt to harm part of her precious house just to frighten me.

The burning bedroom had been the first of more such incidents. At times, parts of the roof would come down, while other times the plaster from the walls would crumble and fall. The curtains would be ripped to shreds. One day, the lintel nearly fell on my head as I entered my room. She wasn't trying to hurt me, but her message was clear.

That was when I started looking for a buyer.

I had told Makrand everything I had experienced, but he ignored my warnings.

I left the house a few days before he moved in, and my new home was cheerful and bright.

I waited for her on my last day in the house, but she never showed herself. I thought of her smile as I left.

After that, I stayed out of town for five months before I returned. Makrand welcomed me to what was now his house. It looked new and beautiful. His wife prepared snacks and we chatted over tea.

Just before I left, Makrand's wife touched my feet for blessings. I was speechless. What could I say? How could I tell Makrand that I recognized the scar on his wife's neck?

MONSOON GUEST

Dusk. Thunderclouds rumbled at the horizon and a sheet of rain drew closer.

That was when the guest arrived. He stepped into the veranda as lightning flashed white, and knocked at the door.

Harinath had been lounging on his chair, muttering shlokas under his breath. He was bare chested, and his stomach moved to the rhythm of the mantras, while his fingers drummed a beat on the armrests. His eyes were closed in deep concentration, only to be disturbed by the knocking.

A thunderclap. The guest knocked again.

Harinath continued with his mantras as the knocking became more aggressive, louder.

Outside, the rain beat down hard, drenching most of the veranda. The guest moved his walking stick from one hand to the other before knocking again – loud and demanding.

Niranjani emerged from one of the rooms and Harinath glanced at her and then at the door – an instruction. Obediently, she opened it. The man on the other side was young and handsome and seemed just as impressed with her appearance as she was with his. She looked radiant. Her tresses flowing down to her waist while her face was fresh like a champa flower, fair and radiant. Each part of her body oozed youth and sensuality.

They both stared at each other for a long, silent moment – which did not go unnoticed by Harinath.

As if singed by Harinath's glare, Niranjani turned away, letting the guest in.

He was a well-built, virile and handsome young man. His dark green eyes were like still lakes – lovely but murky under his wide forehead – as they lingered over Niranjani.

The guest couldn't help but stare at Niranjani. He wondered if she was the owner's wife, even though he looked so much older than her. She could do better, he thought.

As if reading his mind, Niranjani blushed and fidgeted absently with her pallu.

'Sit,' Harinath said to the guest, who took a seat, caressing the ornate handle of his walking stick.

'I've come from Kaldurg,' he said.

Niranjani looked at him with awe and excitement. Kaldurg! Where no one stays or dares to go? That fearsome, isolated fort...

'I'm an archaeologist,' he clarified, sensing her bewilderment. 'You must have expected an old, absent-minded professor. Everyone looks surprised when I tell them what I do.'

'You ... you're returning from Kaldurg?' Harinath asked.

The guest laughed.

'I wonder why Kaldurg evokes such fear,' he said. 'I've even heard locals say Kalmadan, lord of Kaldurg, still roams the land – after four hundred years.'

Niranjani looked as though she had something to say.

The guest continued, 'People believe he's immortal. Apparently, he drains the very youth from young men, prolonging his own life.'

The guest glanced at the doorway. Beyond it, at the end of the road and amongst the trees and their untamed foliage, stood the fort. A dark silhouette against the night sky. The stairs to the imposing structure rose from where the road ended, emerging from thorny branches and entangled vines.

It was old and dilapidated. They would call the place Kalmadan's grave – if they didn't believe he still lived.

'I came here looking for shelter from the rain,' the guest went on. 'I don't have an umbrella and it was threatening to pour at the time. I hope you don't mind me staying here until it stops...'

'Not at all,' Harinath said. 'Stay as long as you like. We can chat.'

The guest could not resist stealing a glance at Niranjani. She was like a flower amongst the thorns. Niranjani, in return, passed him a quick, shy look.

He continued, 'I'm told Kalmadan had a romantic streak. In our research we come across many such tales.'

Harinath was watching Niranjani, who was staring at the archaeologist with provocatively parted lips. 'Tell us more. A story,' she said.

'What? About Kalmadan?' The guest laughed. 'Why only one? I have many.'

'Please, go on,' Niranjani said, moving towards the men.

'Niranjani,' Harinath snapped, 'go make some tea for the guest.'

She got up and left without a word.

The guest stared at her receding figure, her curves.

An awkward silence followed as the men thought of Niranjani. Now they were both wary of each other. The guest believed Niranjani deserved a handsome, young man and not the old Harinath, while Harinath looked at the guest as a wasted youth, not worth his attention.

The storm raged outside, forming puddles in the red soil.

Niranjani returned with the tea and offered the guest a cup.

He couldn't help but stare at her hands, her green bangles. While accepting the cup, his fingers gently brushed against hers.

She quickly withdrew her hand, but Harinath's eyes did not miss anything.

She managed to put the cup down on the table, her fingers shaking nervously.

The guest said, 'Do you want to listen to a story about Kalmadan's tooth? Let me tell you.' He put down his cup and reached for his walking stick, caressing the handle as he spoke. 'It was nearly four hundred years ago. Kalmadan was alive, feeding on the youth of his victims. Did you know he did that with a sword?'

'Sword?' Niranjani uttered. 'But if he still alive, he can't be roaming around with a sword, can he? He must have replaced it with something else…'

A brief silence.

The guest went on, 'One day Kalmadan was invited to an old sardar's house for dinner. The sardar was honoured to host such a prestigious guest.'

The guest seemed to enjoy telling this story. He made sweeping gestures, setting the walking stick aside. Niranjani was engrossed and Harinath too seemed interested in what he had to say.

Many, many years ago.

The sound of hooves grew louder. Soon, the riders stopped at the gates of Sardar Shrimani's haveli, a small fortress. The large doors opened slowly and a drawbridge was lowered over the moat.

Word travelled quickly and the sardar walked to the gates.

One of the horses reared and neighed and the rider dismounted. He wore a black robe. It was Kalmadan.

His eyes met with a particularly beautiful pair, which lowered as they made contact. It was the sardar's wife. She blushed at the sight of him: a handsome young man. He looked strong. Powerful.

Kalmadan touched the hilt of his sword, as was his habit. He wondered how such a lovely woman managed to live in that little fortress they called a haveli, when she deserved the halls of Kaldurg.

He would soon have to use his weapon, but with caution. After all, no one knew the true nature of his sword, which had conquered death itself.

It was a grand feast, with platter after overladen platter offering delicacies both local and exotic. But Kalmadan was distracted. She had filled his goblet with wine and her fingers brushed against his ever so gently.

Mere contact with her flesh had almost made him tremble. He would have to act soon.

When the feast was over, the sardar showed him to his room. It was grand and had a red carpet.

His host slumped into a chair in a drunken stupor. When he opened his eyes, Kalmadan was towering over him, a sword in each hand. 'A gift for your hospitality,' he said.

The sardar slurred, 'My … my pleasure, Kalmadan.'

The sardar then noticed the serpent head on the hilt. He was mesmerized by the twin emeralds – the eyes of the snake. He stared, entranced.

The rider left the fortress. Crossing the moat, he turned to see a hand waving at him from a window.

'What happened next?' Niranjani asked.

'The sardar woke up in the middle of the night,' the guest went on. 'He remembered the sword offered to him with thanks. He reached for it...'

As the guest gestured for effect, his walking stick fell over and rolled towards Niranjani's chair. She picked it up and admired the handle. 'It's so beautiful!'

'It's my constant companion. It helps me when I climb these hills and mountains. But your husband can have it.'

Niranjani looked at her husband and asked, 'Well?'

Harinath was silent for a moment. The guest, realizing that Harinath may be hesitant, said, 'You may keep it. It is not an expensive piece.'

Harinath nodded. 'Thanks,' he said, reaching for it. He couldn't help but stare at it, caress it.

'So what happened next?' she asked.

'Sardar Shrimani picked up the sword,' the guest continued. 'Except for a lamp burning in a corner, the room was dark – but the eyes of the serpent-headed hilt gleamed and, as he stared, he noticed it ... the flicking of a forked tongue.

'He thought it was the wine playing tricks on his mind. Still, he couldn't help but stare at the hilt. This time, the head moved. He closed his eyes against what he thought was merely the effect of alcohol. That was when he felt it slither over his hand.

'When he opened his eyes, there was no sword. He was holding a black snake. He was too stunned to scream.'

'Oh my god...' Niranjani blurted.

'The snake bit him – once, twice. A third time. And then it slithered away, all the way back to Kalmadan who caressed it and then kissed it – drawing in the precious youth the snake had stolen from the sardar with every bite. No doubt the man was dead.

'Kalmadan made plans to visit the fortress the next day to offer his condolences. The woman would be his, soon – and she would have no way of knowing what he had done, now that the snake had turned back into the sword at his side.'

A shiver ran down Niranjani's spine. She had never heard such a story and wondered how anyone could be that cruel. Then she put herself in the sardar's wife's place, and suddenly, the story became strangely exciting.

She looked at the silhouette of Kaldurg, framed by the doorway. It comforted her for some reason, like an old, forgotten home.

The rain continued to pour and lighting flashed between thunderclaps. She relished the idea of losing herself in a handsome stranger's embrace, even though it scared her.

'I must leave now.'

His words shook her out of her reverie. 'Huh?' she muttered.

'I must leave now,' he repeated. 'I can't wait here all night, after all.'

The words hurt. She didn't want him to leave, not with the desire he had kindled.

'Why don't you take an umbrella? You can return it tomorrow,' she said.

She turned to look at Harinath, waiting for his consent. He nodded and she handed their guest an umbrella.

The guest smiled as if they had shared a secret. Now he could return the next day.

'I will come over tomorrow,' he said, adding, 'to return this, of course.'

With that, he stepped into the rain.

The rain did not stop.

Niranjani leaned against a pillar, lost in thought. A light caught her attention. It was Harinath, standing there with a lamp. He could see desire, even lust in her eyes. His own burned like embers.

'Do you really believe I can't tell what you're thinking?'

Unable to face him or his penetrating glare, she turned away.

Harinath took hold of her chin and turned her head to face him, 'Don't try to play games with me! You're planning to run away with him, aren't you?'

'No,' she shouted. 'Please, leave me alone!'

A flash of lighting was followed by thunder.

Harinath picked up the stick left by the stranger. Niranjani tried to move away, but he blocked her path with it. Then he raised it, threatening to strike her.

'Why? Don't you like this any more? I thought it was a gift for you,' he screamed, waving it around.

The flickering lamp made the shadows dance. He continued, 'You were planning to run away, weren't you? Who's going to save you now? That stranger?'

Niranjani screamed as Harinath raised the stick once more. It wasn't the walking stick that terrified her. She saw a snake slither towards him from a dark corner. He tossed the stick aside and picked up the snake, kissing it and draining it of all the youth and vitality it had collected.

She watched on in horror as it turned back into the object she had unwittingly given the stranger – the umbrella.

THE SWING

Back in the day, women were forced to depend on others. If your husband was a teacher, life revolved around school, and if he was a doctor it was the hospital he worked at.

I began reflecting on these things because of that swing. But that was later. Let me start at the beginning.

It all began many years ago, back when I couldn't imagine myself with a son of marriageable age.

I did not study much. Girls my age did go to college, but I was not the studious type. That was why my father decided that I should get married. It would also take the burden off his shoulders.

But for some strange reason, my marriage kept getting delayed. Many prospective bridegrooms would come home and see me, and then decide not to take the discussion further. Each had their own reasons. It got harder as I got older.

We belonged to Dhule and I was keen to get married in a small town. I would not have minded Dhule itself but my father was looking for prospective bridegrooms all over the place. I was hoping he wouldn't find someone in Bombay. I would have hated that. I was fine with some place like Pune or Nashik, but not Bombay. The crowd, the stifling weather! It was not a place I wanted to live in.

My father seemed delighted when he found a prospective bridegroom in Nashik. The man's family had seen my photograph and had agreed to a meeting. Our horoscopes indicated a good match. He was a professor in Nashik and promised my father that he would take care of my further education.

Finally, the wedding day arrived.

I began dreaming of the place that would soon be my home. I had met my future husband once, but in my dreams I could picture the house. It was a huge place, what they called a 'wada' in Nashik. A small mansion with a courtyard. It wasn't very old, but it wasn't well maintained either. The best part about it was the swing in the courtyard. It had brass chains and a wooden seat. One could swing on it for hours.

Soon, I was familiar with the nooks and corners of the house, without having actually stepped into it. I had roamed the house a thousand times, watered the tulsi plant, lit lamps in the evening and enjoyed the swing. Already I loved a place that I hadn't even seen.

I could boast about 'my house in Nashik' to each of my friends. And then, one fine day, just four days before my wedding, we got the news of the bridegroom's aunt's death. They had to postpone the wedding. There were rumours of me being bad luck for the family.

My mother had to pack all my new clothes and jewellery in a trunk and wait for a new date. We had no other option. After all, his aunt was a very close relative and we could not insist on a wedding when a death had occurred in the family.

Soon, all the excitement was renewed as a new date was decided upon. But it was short-lived. Three days before their arrival at Dhule, we found out that the bridegroom had met with an accident. He had escaped with a fractured leg, but would be bedridden for almost six months.

I cried my heart out. I was worried for him. Worried that he would be paralyzed.

Then the murmurs started. The bridegroom recovered after a few months but the family seemed reluctant to re-engage in the conversation regarding our marriage. They kept making excuses to avoid a meeting. I was sure they believed I was responsible for their recent misfortunes. As expected, after a few months of silence, they called off the engagement.

My father went back to looking for a new bridegroom. Finally, my fears were realized. My future husband, working in the postal department, was based in Bombay.

It was a nice four-bedroom house. It was old yet spacious, with a large drawing room and a small swing in the veranda. They wanted a strong, sturdy female to look after the house; not a delicate little thing. It might be why they chose me.

To be honest, I led a happy life there. I had nothing to complain about, and I soon had a son. We were a happy family.

I forgot the old days, and the insult of being rejected. I was even enjoying myself until I had that dream.

I dreamt I had landed in the professor's house in Nashik. I was standing in the courtyard and looking at the swing. I had a strong urge to sit on it, and I did. Its creaking sounded loud in the dead silence of the night, but I enjoyed myself.

I woke up to the sounds in my room in Bombay. I felt strange. Had I really walked into that house in my dreams? I wondered how I could have done that, knowing I had never seen the place.

I brushed aside my fears.

Within a fortnight, I had the same dream. I was not scared this time. I decided to walk up the stairs leading to the rooms at the upper level. The rooms were spacious and airy. The house seemed well kept. I came back to the courtyard and enjoyed the swing for a while. As I sat with my eyes closed, I heard someone shouting, 'Who is it?' It was the professor's voice. I could see someone walking into the courtyard, but before I could get a clearer look, I woke up.

I felt odd the next morning. I vaguely recalled that the professor was partially handicapped. Which meant he had never fully recovered from the accident. I wondered whether it was proper for a married woman like me to have such dreams. After all, I was happily married. My domestic life was smooth and without any troubles. I had never regretted not marrying the professor. So why did I keep dreaming of that house? Why did I feel a great sense of peace when I sat on that swing?

I had never felt such happiness in my house in Bombay.

Something was wrong, but I decided to ignore the guilt I was feeling. I hadn't cheated on my husband, and no one could decide what they dreamed.

The dream recurred. Always, it would be past midnight, and I would roam the house, open doors, look into rooms, check the taps for running water. And, of course, I would enjoy the swing.

The occupants had started getting used to my midnight presence. The professor tried to intimidate me the first couple of times, but he too gave up. His wife had screamed in fear when she first saw me, but soon realized I meant no harm. I could never speak with them, and if I tried, I would wake up.

This went on for years. I had one son, Dinanath, while the professor in Nashik had two children. His elder one, a son, was of the same age as Dinu and was named Madhu, while the younger, a daughter, was Leelu. I had seen them a few times and they weren't afraid of me.

Years passed by. The children had grown up. We too were getting older. Dinanath was working now and we were receiving marriage proposals.

I wondered whether we could send our proposal to Leelu. Of course, I had only seen her in my dreams. I didn't even know if the professor actually had a daughter. But the idea of my son marrying into the family and visiting the house of my dreams was too tempting.

I managed to find a distant relative in Nashik. I had to make some effort to describe the family ... He was a professor, slightly handicapped, with a son and daughter. I felt foolish later. What if the house was not what I imagined? What if there was no swing?

Soon, I received word from my relative: 'Please come to Nashik and meet the family.'

Dinanath was trying to make all kinds of excuses to avoid going to Nashik, but I was determined. He finally relented.

Would you believe me if I said the house was exactly the way I had seen it in my dreams? I knew each and every corner of it! Every bit.

We were welcomed by the professor and his wife. They looked shocked to see me. I could see the recognition in their eyes. They looked at each other but did not say anything.

I said, in order to start a conversation, 'The room upstairs ... looks like you are using it well!'

I then realized what I had said.

'But of course! The children are grown up, you see. They need that extra space,' the professor replied calmly.

Dinu asked, 'Aai, how do you know about the room upstairs?'

It was time I confessed. 'I know each and every corner of this house. For the past twenty-seven years, I have been visiting this place in my dreams.'

At that moment, Leelu came in with the tea. Seeing me, her hand trembled. Somehow, she managed to put down the tray.

'She's surprised to see you,' the professor explained. 'She's been seeing you ever since she was a child. We never thought you were alive. We just assumed you were a harmless ghost. It was quite a shock, frankly, to see you in person today.'

I did not say anything. I stood up and patted Leelu's back. She was still recovering from the shock. I said, 'There is no need to be afraid. Why don't you show me around your house?'

She took me around. It was the first time I was actually seeing the house in person and while awake. Each and every corner was as I remembered.

I wanted her to be my daughter-in-law.

We expressed our wish to have our son marry their daughter. Dinu too had liked the girl. But a girl hardly has a say in her future. The professor declined. Perhaps he didn't want his daughter to marry the son of a woman who roamed his house like a ghost.

I never dreamt of the house gain. After all, my wish had been fulfilled – I got my chance to see the place. Of course, it could also be because I was offended.

We got Dinanath married to a girl from Bombay. Within a few weeks, we received news of Leelu's engagement and marriage. She was to marry a man from Dhule.

It was only yesterday that I woke up in the middle of the night. I could hear the swing in our veranda.

I SEE VIKRAM

Nirmala rushed into my room. 'I have to tell you something!' she said.

I was about to doze off, but this seemed important. 'What about?'

'It's about Nitin.'

'Nitin?

This was no surprise. He was seven, after all – most kids that age drive their mothers crazy with pranks and disobedience. I didn't want to play the tough parent, but she looked worried. Scared.

'The other day I saw him talking to someone at the gate. It looked like he was trying to invite a friend in. I couldn't see who he was talking to, but it must have been a friend who was reluctant to come over.'

'Did you find out who it was?'

'I asked Nitin. He said his name was Vikram.'

'And?'

'Well, it happened again on a different day, so I asked Nitin why this friend wouldn't come in.

'"I don't know. I asked but he refuses," was all Nitin said. Then, one day, Nitin came home very late. I asked him why and all he said was "I was playing with Vikram."'

'Then it must be classmate,' I said.

'No. I asked,' Nirmala said. 'He's not from his school. I think he meets him after school. At the gate.'

'And that bothers you because...?'

'It's strange. Their friendship has developed so fast, he even has extra food packed in his lunchbox. Sometimes, he gives his toys away. His favourite toys.'

'How is that abnormal?'

'It's not, I agree. But shouldn't we know who our child's friends are?'

She knew my answer, but she'd always been a bit paranoid, fussing over Nitin's hygiene, nutrition and whatnot. She'd call the doctor over the slightest health concern and read up on possible illnesses. True, Nitin was our only child, but sometimes she'd worry too much over nothing.

She went on. 'I tried getting some more information out of him, but his answers are so vague. If I ask where he lives, all Nitin says is "too far". Although, he did mention that Vikram's clothes look unwashed, and that he's not well dressed. I don't think he's from a well-off, educated family.'

That was another one of her hang-ups. She wanted Nitin to mingle with children from the same social class as us. I agreed to some extent – I didn't want him picking up bad habits from slum children.

'I've been insisting, but he still hasn't brought that boy over. Could he have made it all up? Taking food, and toys to—'

'Nirmala! Let it go. We should have some faith in the boy.'

I decided to check out who this Vikram was. I asked the schoolteachers, but they couldn't recall anyone by that name. After school, I waited outside the gate.

As soon as the bell rang, Nitin came running to the gate. I hid behind a tree and watched him as he started walking towards home. I followed him for a while and then took a shortcut to reach home before he did. When he got home, I asked whether he had met Vikram. He said, 'Yes, we walked back together.' When I asked him where Vikram waited for him after school, he said he had been standing right outside the school gate. I wasn't sure if he was making it up or actually had seen his friend.

'Yesterday he stayed home – not feeling well,' Nirmala said. 'I asked him whether he wanted to go out and play, but he refused. Suddenly, he shouted, "Aai, Vikram is here! I'll go down". Without waiting for my response, he went to the gate. I watched from our window. There was no one at the gate. But Nitin was talking to someone. Animatedly.'

That shook me up. 'Are you sure there was no one?'

'Absolutely no one! Why does he lie to us?'

'Is he just mumbling to himself or has he come up with an imaginary friend?' I was worried and decided to have a chat with Nitin.

That evening I asked him, 'Nitin, Vikram is a friend of yours, isn't he?'

'A close friend.'

'Why don't you call him over?'

'He doesn't want to come here. He's a free bird.'

'Free bird?'

'He doesn't like to stay home and roams around all the time. He loves it, he says.'

'Is he fair like you?'

'Not at all. He's really dark.'

I wondered if Nitin had created a character to be the opposite of him. An alter ego of sorts – one who roamed free, not disciplined by an anxious mother. A boy who could live life on his own terms.

'And you know, Baba? He has a lovely black dog. It is so intelligent, you know ...' Nitin went on.

The next morning, I took Nitin to a psychologist.

I had briefed the doctor on his situation. The doctor asked Nitin a number of questions. Finally, I had a chance to speak with him privately, after he was done examining Nitin.

'There's nothing to worry,' he said, smiling. 'The boy is perfectly normal. He is a little sensitive and has created an imaginary friend. He is an only child, after all. Sometimes, children create their own playmates if they don't have a sibling. Sometimes, they start believing their creation is real. But they get over it when they grow up. Don't worry.'

I soon realized that the doctor was wrong. Nitin did not forget Vikram. On the contrary, their friendship deepened. They would meet often, at times even when Nitin was with me or Nirmala. He began seeing Vikram more often. It was impossible to believe that Nitin was imagining something, the way he would talk and respond to Vikram. Barring his interaction with the imaginary boy, he behaved like a normal child.

Vikram needed to disappear. But how?

'Baba,' Nitin said one day as I was reading a newspaper. 'Vikram wants to go back.'

'Go back? Where?'

'He didn't say. But he wants me to go with him. Can I, Baba?'

That was scary. Where was Vikram asking him to go?

'He misses his dog, Kalu. He says he could go see him. He said, if I went along, the three of us could be together and have fun.'

I didn't want to scare Nirmala by telling her about our conversation, but it had left me shaken.

I decided to find out about the places Nitin had visited over the past year – ever since he had started seeing and talking to Vikram. At the school, I asked if there had been an ex-student named Vikram. But the records did not show any such name.

In the meanwhile, Nitin would keep pestering me with that unsettling question. 'Can I go with Vikram? He's calling me.'

One day, Nitin showed me a photograph of Vikram. It was from one of his school trips. There he was, standing with a black dog. Nitin and Vikram stood next to each other, smiling into the camera. There he was, just as Nitin described.

So he did exist. But why couldn't we see him?

Nirmala couldn't believe her eyes when I showed her the photo. She was sure this was a different boy whose picture Nitin was using to cover up his lie.

I was reluctant to let go of the small thread of hope the picture had given me. I decided to investigate further. On enquiring at the school, I discovered that Nitin and his classmates had gone for a school picnic a couple of years ago. It was a place called Kalyangadh, a fort in the hills nearby. The photo was from that picnic. The boy in the picture must have been a local.

The next day, I arrived at the village at the base of the fort.

By the time I got to the fort, the sun had set and it was getting dark. Silhouetted against the rapidly darkening sky, the fort looked menacing. There was no one around. I could see the light from oil lamps in the village. It was a dull, depressing evening.

I stopped at the first house on the edge of the village and looked in. An old lady was busy making her dinner. I asked, 'Which is Vikram's house?'

A dog wailed in the distance, startling me.

I repeated my question, but got no response. Seeing her blank stare I explained, 'A young boy, maybe around ten or so.'

'Oh, that boy,' she said. She gestured to a young boy sitting in a corner of the hut and said, 'Take this gentleman to Sawle's house.'

I followed the boy to a small hut. The howling dog sounded very close. His was a mournful and unsettling howl.

I asked, as soon as a woman stepped out of the house, 'Where is Vikram?'

A sob escaped her lips. She said, covering her mouth partially with the edge of her sari, 'He ... it's been ten months since...' She disappeared into the darkness of the inner room without another word. I was stunned. I turned and left immediately. The boy followed me and gave me some more information.

Vikram had died ten months ago, having slipped and fallen off a cliff. His dog Kalu still searched for him, howling with grief. People started saying that Kalu could see Vikram and that they roamed around together. Kalu had, since then, thinned down considerably and looked like a bag of bones. Now, he would just sit in one place and wail.

The next morning, as I waited at the bus stand, the boy came running and announced, 'Kalu died last night.'

Fear pierced my heart.

I got home to find an excited Nitin, jumping with joy. He said, 'You know, Baba, I really enjoyed our game this evening; me, Vikram and Kalu. He was finally able to get Kalu last night!'

I was shivering. I asked, unable to keep my voice steady, 'Nitin, did you meet Vikram on that school picnic trip ten months ago?'

'Yes,' Nitin said, without hesitation. 'I had pleaded for him to come home. I remember that.'

'It's different with people who are … alive. You can't stay friends with them after they die. And Vikram … is dead. He fell off a cliff and died.'

Nitin said nothing. I wasn't even sure he understood what I had said. But his expression turned serious.

The next day, Nitin did not return from school. I enquired at the school after waiting for him for a long time.

I was told he had left a little earlier than usual. The class teacher said, 'He said he was not feeling well.'

'Why did you allow him to go alone?'

'He said his friend was accompanying him.'

Vikram! My heart began pounding in my chest.

Nirmala and I took the next bus to Kalyangadh.

By the time we got there, it was night. There was complete silence everywhere.

A crowd had gathered at the base of the cliff. I rushed down there, pushing my way through the crowd.

There he was – lying in a pool of blood.

Some said they saw him running towards the cliff and then jumping off before anyone could react.

I knew Vikram had finally managed to convince Nitin to join him.

While writing this story, I heard a dog howling outside. I stopped and rushed to the window. Nirmala, standing behind me, asked, 'What happened?'

'Don't you hear a dog howling?'

'No!' She seemed a little surprised. She looked out of the window and then walked away, shrugging as she said, 'You've been acting strange ever since Nitin died. You should try and get some sleep.'

But I couldn't look away from the window, because I could see them out there, in the moonlight. Two boys and a dog.

FOLLOWED

Dr Diwekar always experienced the strange feeling of being followed while driving. He kept an eye on the rear-view mirror, always suspicious.

He had been wrong before, but this time he was certain the man on the motorcycle was tailing him.

Most cars turned one way or the other at the crossroads, but he drove straight and continued down a lonely stretch of road. So did the man on the motorcycle.

That road was always quiet with only a few cars heading to the hospital it led to. On this evening, he and the motorcyclist were alone.

Uneasy, he remembered Saptarshi, who always rode a motorcycle.

He could see, in the mirror, that the mysterious man was wearing a black shirt, black pants.

Dr Saptarshi always wore black, as if it were a fashion statement. God knows what Saptarshi thought of himself. He was a good-looking man, but put too much thought into his appearance, focusing on the contrast of a white coat on black. *Show off.*

The memory of Dr Saptarshi made Dr Diwekar uncomfortable. He had been on edge for a fortnight – jittery for no apparent reason.

He reflected on the irony of a doctor being unable to determine the cause of his own discomfort.

The biker was closer now and was clearly visible in the rear-view mirror. Dr Diwekar sat up with a jolt.

The same lean body. His hair blowing in the wind ... *Dr Saptarshi? Impossible.*

Dr Saptarshi had died on the operating table a fortnight ago.

The two doctors had been close friends.

They graduated from medical school and joined the hospital, both at the same time.

They were of the same age but the corpulent and balding Dr Diwekar had a more commanding personality while Dr Saptarshi was the attractive, fashionable one. No one would believe that they had been classmates.

Both were unmarried and would spend their free time playing cards, watching movies. They agreed on most issues, and their hobbies were similar.

Days went by peacefully. Until Neelima Sarang arrived at the hospital.

Dr Diwekar brushed off the memories and focussed on the biker behind him.

He wondered if he was being paranoid. After all, a lot of young men wore dark clothes. And long hair was all the rage. In fact, if Dr Diwekar's hairline hadn't receded...

He checked himself. Was he trying to convince himself it wasn't Saptarshi? The man was dead – end of subject.

He focussed on the lonely road, snaking its way up the hill with water gleaming on one side, reflecting the dull sunlight.

Unable to shake the driver, both from behind him and from his thoughts, he decided to let him overtake his car.

Dr Diwekar slowed down and waited.

The motorcycle did not overtake him. He remained behind the car.

Neelima was a sweet girl whose poise set her apart.

She had joined as a nurse and carried herself with dignity and authority, but without arrogance. She also had a sweet voice and a pretty, dimpled smile, which had caught Dr Diwekar's attention.

Dr Diwekar preferred to stay away from all the drama that came with affairs at the workplace, having heard enough about them through the grapevine. Instead, he and Saptarshi would amuse themselves by joking about all the doctors and nurses they deemed unattractive or incompetent.

Neelima Sarang had burst his little drama-free bubble.

Diwekar and Saptarshi soon stopped making crass jokes about the nursing staff. Their gossip was replaced with praise for Neelima's intelligence and efficiency. They would invite her to join them for tea and coffee. She was articulate and could talk on a wide variety of subjects.

She never pretended to be like one of the doctors, though, and never shirked work. Her traits made her even more attractive to Diwekar, and he soon realized he was in love with her.

He was unlikely to meet someone like Neelima again – of that he was certain. She had walked into his life and he was not going to let the opportunity slip away.

He decided to propose to her. It would be an evening he would remember for the rest of his life.

Christmas eve.

The hospital was run by a Christian mission and Christmas was celebrated with a staff party followed by a ball. There would be emergency calls, doctors' shifts, but the party and the fun would not stop.

It was on such a lovely evening, in the hospital's garden and under swaying lamps, that Diwekar was to ask Neelima to marry him. He imagined she would smile, blush and softly say yes.

Dr Diwekar put on his black jacket and pinned on a white rosebud. He was spraying perfume over his coat when the bell rang and, pushing the door open, Dr Saptarshi rushed in.

He was, as usual, dressed nattily with a few top buttons of his shirt undone. His hair covered half his forehead and his blue eyes were bright and radiant.

'Aren't you going to the party?' Diwekar asked.

'Believe me, I could really use some rest and relaxation. How about a few drinks here, away from all the people we see every day?'

'I know what you mean, but I should get going. Important work to do.'

'Forget work – it's all you ever talk about,' Saptarshi said, slapping Diwekar on the back. 'And look at you, being all old school with that suit. Come on, let's just hang out here, I want to tell you something.' Saptarshi beamed, clearly elated. 'Guess what? This afternoon, at lunch, I proposed to Neelima. She said yes!'

Diwekar's world came crashing down.

The road turned, and the ocean disappeared behind the trees. He drove up the hill, and for a moment it seemed like the biker was gone.

He heard the bike before he saw it again in his mirror.

Dr Diwekar accelerated. So did the biker. It was not easy to accelerate on the steep slope.

He accelerated further. The bike moved faster still. It was gaining on him, even on the steep slope.

The man was following him – there was no doubt about it.

Diwekar's pulse raced. He didn't know if he was speeding away from danger or straight towards it.

The man in black was nearing the car. The purring of the motorcycle reverberated in the silence around them.

He wandered aimlessly through the crowd at the Christmas party. He felt a sudden urge to return to his room and lock himself away from the world.

Recovering from the initial shock, he steadied himself and stretched out his hand, putting on a fake smile. 'Congratulations!'

He was dressed up for the party. And he could not miss it. Saptarshi was with him and was almost floating with joy. There was no stopping him, the way he danced, got drunk and blabbered constantly.

Diwekar stood in a corner, holding a glass and watching the others enjoy themselves. Music played and the lanterns nodded in the wind. Everyone had put on their paper party hats and their voices mingled in a cacophony of Christmas and New Year greetings. All Diwekar could do was play along while yearning for his room.

Neelima walked over and took a seat across from him.

Her expression was calm, he noticed, not excited. He wondered if he was imagining that and was simply in denial of that fact that she could be happy with another man.

'Why are you sitting here alone? Not feeling well?' She sounded concerned.

Diwekar detected affection in her tone. If only he could have enjoyed it for the rest of his life.

Gulping down his drink, Diwekar blurted, without meeting her eyes, 'Congratulations!'

'He already told you?' The dimples returned with her smile, but he looked away, stung by the way she said 'he'.

'Good thing he did. Or else I would have proposed,' he pretended to joke.

'Well, that would have been a tough choice,' she answered with a laugh.

Diwekar's face lit up at her response. She got up and walked away, but his gaze lingered over her.

She had given him hope.

Those words ... She loved him, even if not with the same intensity with which he loved her. But nevertheless! Notwithstanding her feelings for Saptarshi, she would have, had he proposed, said yes! She loved both, was affectionate to both and liked their company. Why else would she ask about his health?

Neelima would have loved me if it weren't for Saptarshi. I'm sure of it.

If only Saptarshi was not around.

Diwekar imagined a world without Saptarshi. His path was clear. Neelima was his and his alone.

The next moment, he was shaken out of his reverie. What if he made Saptarshi disappear?

Tchah! He shook the thought out of his head. He was not a murderer. Besides ... it wouldn't be easy.

Troubled by such disturbing thoughts, Diwekar rushed out of the party.

Four days later, Saptarshi died. He succumbed to injuries from a motorcycle accident. His motorcycle was damaged beyond recognition.

It was quite clear then that the motorcycle following his car could not be Saptarshi's, Diwekar tried convincing himself.

And that man – how could the man be him?

But the resemblance...

Diwekar's mind was in shambles with all the unnerving thoughts playing in a loop over and over and over again – until his knuckles were white and a joyless grin stretched across his face.

The car raced uphill with the motorcycle inching closer by the minute. The whirring of the bike sounded like a swarm of angry bees.

The trees were a blur now and the wind and bike engine buzzed in Diwekar's ears as he continued to push the accelerator.

The motorcycle was almost in the air.

No! He would never be forgiven. He wouldn't be spared. He had to escape, even if it meant going faster and faster and—

The world went upside down, blurring, rolling faster and faster and—

Darkness.

◉

Even after the crash, the wheels of Dr Diwekar's upturned car continued to spin for a long time.

When he opened his eyes, all he saw was a white wall.

He looked down and noticed bandages wound around him, restricting his movement like blinkers on a horse. There were familiar smells and a calendar on the wall.

He was at the hospital.

What happened to me?

A painful spasm in his back made him writhe in pain and suddenly it all came back to him.

The wind, the trees, the man on the motorcycle.

How did he escape the rider's clutches? It had surely been him.

How am I still alive?

Diwekar stared at the white wall.

◉

Neelima had fainted when she heard of Dr Saptarshi's accident.

She used to warn him against speeding. But he would not listen. He was passionate about everything he loved, whether it was Neelima or the bike or the thrill of speeding.

He was on his way to the hospital at his usual fast pace when a goods truck came from the other side. As he tried to weave his way past it, the bike skidded, and he fell. Luckily he survived. But he suffered a serious head injury.

He was admitted at the hospital where they worked.

First, Neelima cried her heart out. After a while, the nurse in her took charge. She was determined to save his life.

An emergency operation, a brain surgery, was to be performed on Saptarshi.

When he looked at her before going into the operating theatre, tears flowed down her cheeks. She smiled, holding his hand gently before he was wheeled away for the procedure.

Diwekar said, looking at Neelima, 'Please! I know you're capable and that you love him, but you're emotionally compromised right now. Please send another nurse.'

The operation theatre was ready to receive the patient. It was to be performed by Dr Singhani, who was reputed in the field and had performed many such operations. Dr Diwekar was to assist him.

The only one sitting outside was Neelima. She counted every minute and wished she could be inside. But she had full faith in Diwekar.

Finally, after what seemed like an eternity, the doors of the operating theatre opened. Dr Singhani came out followed by Dr Diwekar. They all walked away without even glancing at her.

For a moment she stood still, not knowing what to do.

Then it dawned on her. Saptarshi had died on the operating table.

The silence around Diwekar was shattered by Neelima, who walked in wearing her nurse's uniform.

No one wanted to speak. They both looked at each other, their eyes moist.

She asked in a soft voice, 'Are you feeling better?'

Dr Diwekar thanked his stars that he had survived and was able to hear her voice. It was full of concern and love.

He smiled.

She continued, 'I'm surprised! You drive so carefully. What happened today?'

He wanted to tell her everything: that Saptarshi had chased him to the brink of death.

But he checked himself. Even if she believed him, she wouldn't understand Saptarshi's motive.

Diwekar was silent. Neelima said, staring vacantly, 'It's like I'm a jinx. First that accident and now you.'

A small hope sprung in Diwekar's mind. She was worried about him. She was concerned.

He would propose to her soon, but he would have to be sensitive about it. He had to let her grieve.

There was no doubt in his mind that she would be his, now that Saptarshi was no more. Then it dawned on him: Saptarshi must have chased him because he knew what he was planning to do. Though dead, the man was still jealous.

The very idea terrified him. There was nothing to stop the dead man from trying to kill him again. Sooner or later, Diwekar's luck would run out.

'We need to perform a small operation on your spine,' Neelima announced.

'Dr Gadkari, the surgeon, should be in by noon. Don't worry.'

At noon, Diwekar was wheeled into surgery.

Diwekar asked that Neelima be present for the procedure. He felt comfortable knowing she would be close.

A silence fell over the room. The only thing Diwekar could hear was the ticking of the clock and the breathing of those present.

There had been a similar silence then. Just the sound of clock and their breathing.

He lay on the table – the man who had been his best friend. The one Neelima was to wed.

Surgeon Singhani and his serious expression as he snapped on the gloves, frowning over his mask.

The ticking of the clock.

Lying there, Saptarshi looked so different it was hard to imagine a smile on that once cheerful face.

Silence. Diwekar lay on his table and his mind raced.

The light above and the darkness around.

Why am I scared? What of? The man on the motorcycle. He must have vanished when my car finally crashed. But it was surely him. Waiting to take my life.

Surgeon Gadkari indicated for the anaesthetist to begin. Diwekar stared at the anaesthetist, and then he noticed it: the resemblance.

The blue eyes. The black collar beneath the white gown. It was Saptarshi. *He's going to kill me!*

'Help! Help!' he screamed. 'He's Saptarshi. He wants to kill me, because I killed him! I murdered him! I gave him an overdose of anaesthesia and now he wants revenge!'

A deep, cold silence followed.

◉

It was a quiet, sad evening, when Diwekar regained consciousness.

Someone was sitting near his pillow.

It was not Neelima. It was not Saptarshi. It was someone else – a young man who resembled Saptarshi. A nurse stood close to them.

The nurse came closer as he opened his eyes. Pointing at the young man she said, 'Meet Dr Ashtikar. He joined in place of Dr Saptarshi.'

Diwekar noticed that Ashtikar was wearing a black shirt over dark trousers.

'He joined this morning. He was late and was rushing over to the hospital when he saw you speeding and, finally, crashing. He brought you in.'

Dr Ashtikar smiled. 'Now that she's got the introductions covered, I thought I'd reassure you that I'm not Dr Saptarshi. And I definitely didn't give you an overdose.'

Diwekar smiled.

'Of course, your admission of guilt has raised a lot of questions. Neelima was planning to go to the police, but I don't think the hospital will allow her to do that. The management needs to take into account the reputation of the hospital. The whole episode is going to be devastating for you, of course, but at the moment you need all your strength to recover.'

Diwekar wondered how it would help even if he were to recover. It was clear that Neelima would not want to see him ever again. He would be labelled a murderer. The nurse walked away.

'I did not give you an overdose. If I wanted to kill you, I could have hit you on the head while you were still in the wreckage. No one would have suspected.' His next words pierced Diwekar's heart. 'May you live long to repent your sins.'

Diwekar listened to Ashtikar, squirming all the while. He was destined to suffer for the rest of his life.

'Remember your oath. As a doctor, you must do no harm. I kept you alive, doctor, for the same reason,' Ashtikar said, as he laughed out loud.

Diwekar barely heard him. Instead, he was staring at his face.

'By the way, you were right, back there. The real Ashtikar is at home. Luckily, no one's seen him before, so the switch was easy. Which is lucky, since I haven't quite figured out how to change form.' Saptarshi guffawed. 'Live and let live, Doctor ... for the dead are quite terrifying.'

With that, Saptarshi faded into thin air. But his laughter lingered on.

BETWEEN STRANGERS

Chandrakant closed his eyes, exhausted. He had been at his desk, working from morning until late evening, while his colleagues arrived, worked, talked and finally left.

By the time he stepped out of the office, he was too tired to return the doorman's salute. His driver opened the car door for him and he was on his way home.

At home he was greeted by his children. 'Daddy's home, Daddy's home!'

Savita managed to tear the children away from him and helped him take off his coat. 'You seem very tired today,' she said.

'Huh...' was all he mumbled, even though his head was buzzing with questions: Why the fatigue? Where was that old enthusiasm for work? Why wasn't Savita just as tired?

He wondered if age had caught up with him. *Forty isn't that old ... is it?*

He had no answers. He took a seat at the dining table and sipped at his tea. He had one more cup, which Savita poured him lovingly from a delicate porcelain kettle. He shook his head when she got a plate of poha and walked up the stairs to the terrace. He sank into an easy chair when Ramnath got him the *Times*, which he promptly put on the table as he tried to relax.

It was his favourite chair. He liked that it was big and had a classic design. It was his father's. The moment he sat in it, resting his hands on the broad wooden armrests, he could feel the fatigue melt away.

He glanced at the newspaper, lying there in the last rays of the sun, but was too preoccupied to read. His mind was set on time and its effects – on Savita and himself. She tried hard to look young and attractive, not that he was the strapping young man he had been in college – his grey hair had made sure of that. Watching the sun set, he was lost in thought.

Charulata was sick of lying in bed. Bored stiff, she had been idly staring at the curtains, watching them turn golden with the sunlight beaming through, drawing out their intricate pattern like filigree.

It was no state for a beautiful college student to be in, but there had been no reasoning with the disease that kept her in bed. The weakness was debilitating, but all that the doctors could diagnose was her low blood pressure.

At least her thoughts fluttered about freely, alighting on visions of pretty dresses and scenarios in which she could gallivant and dance and fall in love.

The very thought of romance brought a smile to her face.

She glanced at the door that opened into the garden. She could see the dense creeper running along the wall and the arch above the gate, which was open as usual. Not that many people came that way.

It was as if she were waiting for someone. Of course, none of her friends would do – most were immature, struggling even to grow a moustache. No, she wanted an older man: serious, well built and thoughtful. Someone who would treat her well.

Then she noticed someone standing below the arch.

Curious, she stared at him. It wasn't anyone she knew. But he was striking. She sat up, mesmerized by the image of him against the low, golden clouds. He looked so handsome.

She stood up with an enthusiasm she had not felt in a long time and forgot her weakness. The man started walking towards her. It felt like they knew each other.

He looked middle-aged. The hair on his temples was greying and it added to his personality. He must have been tired but his face was radiant. His confident smile was unlike so many she had seen on the faces of awkward college boys. No, this was a *man*.

Charulata stepped forward eagerly and made her way down the steps to the garden – something she hadn't done in four months. Finally, she looked up in the last rays of the sun and—

He was gone. There was no one there – not in front of her, not even at the gate.

She wondered if her mind was playing tricks on her, but then realized how far she had walked. Something special had happened. She felt refreshed.

Slowly, she made her way back to bed, thinking about the handsome man.

Chandrakant opened his eyes but was not sure where he was.

After a moment his thoughts cleared and he saw Savita's face. He could hear the children shouting, 'Daddy, Daddy!'

He heard a sigh of relief. Savita said to someone standing a little away, probably Ramnath, 'He is conscious.' She asked, 'How are you feeling? Are you okay?'

He could see the terrace wall. The next building, his chair. Then he remembered a different place: a beautiful house with a red roof. There had been a garden … and a girl. A frail girl. Like a painter's imagination on water.

'Do you want to rest in bed?' Savita's voice was sweet with a tinge of coyness. 'You're not well. Come in.'

The children led him by a hand each. It was dark outside, where the lamp was burning like a beacon. Savita helped him to bed, unfolded the blanket.

'You know how scared we were? I thought you'd fainted! You're overworked and really need to rest.'

Chandrakant was silent. He was actually feeling good. Energetic and refreshed even. He kept wondering about the girl. She had approached him. He must have dozed off for just a few minutes and yet the dream was so real ... and beautiful.

Charulata did not mention the vision to her older brother, who had been taking care of her. Still, she wanted to experience it all again, even if it was just a trick her mind had played on her.

At night, Charulata tossed and turned restlessly. The room was stuffy and she walked over to open the door for some fresh air. Outside, the moonlight spread silver over the garden.

Suddenly, she felt something. Somehow, at that very moment, she knew he was there.

She was right. A shiver of anticipation and desire ran up her spine as he reached for her. She walked towards him, overcome by a feeling she could not name. Eagerly she let herself fall into his embrace – and slipped right through him.

She hit the ground and screamed in pain. Within moments her brother rushed out and was by her side. There was no one else.

Chandrakant sat up with a jerk. His body was drenched in sweat.

The dream had recurred, and this time, he was sure the girl knew him. She had been waiting for him and embraced him and … he couldn't remember what happened next.

Savita was awake and staring at his face. He knew he had frightened her again, but she didn't ask questions. He wondered if he should tell her the truth. He couldn't. Instead, he lay awake trying to think of what to do.

Charulata decided to confide in her brother. She regained consciousness in the garden and he helped her to bed. He tucked her in and was about to leave when she called out to him.

'Dada, please stay! I am scared.'

He brought her water and touched her forehead to check for fever. Finally, she found her voice and told him everything.

'Don't worry, Charu,' he said. 'Your weakness is making you hallucinate. Don't worry, you'll get better soon and all of … all of that will stop.'

It sounded as if he was reassuring himself that what she had just described was a figment of her imagination. He sat there until she fell asleep before switching off the lights and walking back to his room. Suddenly, a disturbing thought took hold of him. What if it was real? What if she had actually seen someone?

Had some spirits possessed his sister? She was ill and possibly receptive to such things. He needed to do something. Soon.

The next day, he spoke to the neighbours and older folk about the history of the house. Nothing they said could possibly suggest evil spirits and supernatural activity.

He was not convinced. He started worrying and spent more time looking after her.

Her condition deteriorated. She tried to look strong for her brother, knowing he wouldn't understand why she still waited for the handsome man who had left her feeling so invigorated the first time. But what about Dada? His views were totally different. The very thought troubled her. She was tired of waiting.

Her mind reeled from constantly looking out of the window. It was bright and sunny outside, but the curtains kept the room cool. Glancing at the gate had become a habit. But apart from the golden-yellow sunshine, there was nothing.

Finally, one day, she sensed a presence and turned towards it.

He was standing at her bedside, a smile playing on his lips. His eyes seemed to ask, *'How are you feeling now?'*

She stood up with a sudden surge of energy. She wanted to say, *'I'm feeling great – now that you're here!'*

She was about to say something when her brother came in. For a moment, he was stunned and kept staring at both of them. The moment he saw the figure standing next to his sister, he realized that it was the same middle-aged man Charulata had told him about. The one she had seen the other night…

'Who are you?' Dada asked, gathering his courage.

He did not get a response. It seemed the apparition was unwilling to speak. Or could he simply not hear?

Dada repeated, 'Who are you?'

He realized then that he was speaking to the window. The man was gone.

Chandrakant opened his eyes to see the doctor wiping the sweat off his face.

He had fainted in the middle of a meeting, shocking everyone. The doctor had been summoned and the staff looked worried.

The doctor checked his pulse and blood pressure. 'Everything is normal,' he said. 'There is no need to worry.'

Chandrakant smiled meekly, wondering what he was going through.

The doctor called in to the office and the family doctor both concurred that Chandrakant needed some rest, though there was no cause for worry. He was forced to take leave. His boss insisted.

Savita booked a hotel room at a hill station. The children were to be sent to their aunt's place lest they miss their school. Savita was determined to nurse him back to health.

But Chandrakant wasn't the least bit excited about the trip and was lost in thought. She noticed that his mind was elsewhere, until they finally drove off towards the hill. His eyes lit up when they were finally surrounded by lush green landscapes and breathtaking blue mountains.

Chandrakant wondered if he could close his eyes and go back into his dream.

But the dreams were not as beautiful as before. The girl was lying in bed and had not approached him. And that gentleman – who was he? Her brother?

Suddenly he was snapped out of his reverie. He couldn't believe his eyes – it was the house from his dreams. The yellow one with the red roof. 'Stop!' he shouted. The car screeched to a halt.

Chandrakant got out of the car.

Yes! It was the same house. He recognized the gate, the arch, the flowering creeper.

'Where are you going?' Savita shouted, as she got out of the car and followed him.

Chandrakant walked through the gate and up the steps.

The girl's brother stood there, shocked. He asked, 'You ... you've come back?' His voice was strangely hoarse.

Chandrakant stopped in his tracks. The man looked strange. His dishevelled hair, his bloodshot eyes...

'You've possessed my sister. What do you want now?'

Chandrakant pushed him aside without answering him and walked towards Charulata's room.

'Run! There's is a ghost!' Charulata's brother shouted as he rushed into the garden.

Chandrakant caught him by the arm. 'I'm not a ghost. Here! Look at me carefully,' he shouted.

The brother was speechless.

'I've been seeing you too,' Chandrakant said. 'In my dreams. I've seen this house, you … the girl. I didn't know any of it was real, but believe me – I am.'

'Then … then what's going on?'

'I don't know! They say the mind can … project itself. Thoughts, desires. I don't know.'

Chandrakant made for the room when the brother spoke up, loud and clear.

'You're a few hours too late. She gave up … on you … on everything.'

Chandrakant looked into the room. She lay there on the bed, perfectly still.

He knew that she would never rush towards him again.

VAMPIRE

It was a new moon and close to midnight. I was all alone in the car and on a lonely road, with only a few bungalows along the way, and between them – construction sites littered with building materials.

On the other side of the road was a stretch of flat, barren land with the creek beyond it. I couldn't see the water in the dark.

There was a strong wind blowing and it made driving all the more fun! I increased the speed a little more, and suddenly she stood in front of me. I braked.

A beautiful, young woman dressed in pristine white clothes! She stood right in the middle of the road waving her delicate hands gently.

Her white sari stood out starkly in the pitch darkness of the new moon night. Isn't she scared of asking for a lift from a stranger at this late hour?

I had already stopped the car. She walked slowly towards it.

'Where do you want to go?' I asked.

'Where are you going?' she asked in return with a smile.

'I am going very far. Don't worry, I will drop you home on the way.'

She told me her address.

I smiled and said, 'Oh! Is that it? I'll drop you. Come in.'

I opened the door and she sat next to me. I stole a glance at her just as I started the car. She possessed an unusual beauty, making it difficult to look away from her. She was fair, her eyebrows were arched and her face was flushed. Maybe she was worried.

'I hope I'm not troubling you?' she said in a sweet voice.

'Oh, not at all. On the contrary, I'm happy to have some company,' I said with a chuckle.

She thought I was being courteous, but it was true. She made the lonely drive pleasant. She laughed as if reading my mind. Her laugh was like a melody and her pearl-white teeth glistened when she smiled.

I asked, 'Where were you going at this time of the night?'

She didn't say anything. She was busy winding the window up and said, 'I am feeling cold.'

I repeated my question.

'For a shoot. I was at a shoot in Amrut Studio.'

'What? You're an actress?' My respect for her shot up instantly.

She laughed mirthlessly. 'If I were an actress, would I be thumbing a lift like this? There are producers, directors and cameramen ready with their cars to drop actresses home. I'm just an extra.'

She continued to speak. The road was empty and the ride smooth. I stepped up the speed.

'Amrut Studio is in a corner of the city. It's very difficult to find transport at night. And anyway, who cares about extras like us? Come if you can or get lost!'

I wasn't listening to her. I was more focussed on her gestures and her changing facial expressions while she spoke. Her bluish eyes were sparkling and her blood-red, juicy lips moved seductively.

Why don't these extras wipe out their makeup properly before they leave for home?

'I'm feeling really cold,' she repeated abruptly. 'Even after rolling the windows up. God knows why!' All of a sudden she started shivering. I don't know what she was thinking, but she moved closer to me. Very close.

I placed my left arm around her shoulder. She did not resist.

Just then, her destination arrived and she asked me to stop the car. I strained my eyes in the darkness. There seemed to be an open ground in front of us, with a few houses along its boundary. I soon realized they weren't really houses but haphazardly built walls that looked more like tombstones, only slightly bigger. Someone had lit a fire on the other side of the ground to ward off the cold. The firelight cast strange shadows over her and I marvelled at the contrast of her beauty against the gloomy, destitute, surroundings. She got out of the car and said, 'You can stop here. I'll go on my own from here.' She turned and began walking away. I sat staring at her retreating figure. She swayed like a swan as she gently entered the impoverished settlement, vanishing behind a whitewashed wall.

A beautiful dream disappeared into the darkness of the night...

I drove to the same place the next day, and got there at the same time: midnight.

I stayed in my car, but slowed down to take in the surroundings.

I had a feeling I would see her, and lo and behold: there she was, standing at the same place as yesterday. She waved to me and I stopped. Again, she was in a white sari. Her face looked the same, but more made up. She looked breathtakingly beautiful.

I opened the door and she came in. Again, she sat very close to me. I focussed on the road, but I could feel her eyes on me.

She seemed to be soaking in the very sight of me. A strange attraction seemed to be developing between us. A burning, raging attraction. The heat of the flames could have singed us, but instead it seemed to have a soothing effect. Her thoughts seemed to be drawn towards me and I was getting aroused under the spell.

I stopped the car saying, 'Shall we sit here for a while?'

She pretended to be surprised and asked, 'Here? Now?'

'Yes,' I said. 'Is there a problem?'

'No ... but...' she hesitated.

'People at home – will they be waiting for you?' I asked.

'Home?' She laughed aloud. 'No, nobody is waiting for me. Besides, it's already past midnight.'

I locked the car and both of us started walking. The sea was right in front of us. The beach was rocky. She held my arm tightly and walked carefully over the rocks until we found a place to sit.

The waves came roaring and crashed against the shore. The sound would ebb and pick up again. We sat there in silence, listening to the sea. There was no need for words. It seemed as if we could read each other's thoughts and feelings without speaking.

I gently placed my hand on her shoulder and pulled her into an embrace before kissing her passionately. She threw her head back in pleasure, her hair falling undone. I was captivated by her lips and we lay there on the rocks for some time, listening to the sea grow calmer.

Finally we returned to our senses and got up. We dusted our clothes off and walked hand-in-hand towards the car.

I started the car, raced towards her settlement and stopped at the same place as last night. This time, I got out too. 'Please, don't come. I'll go on my own,' she said in an unsteady voice.

I quietly went back and sat in the car.

On the third day, I returned to the same place. At the stroke of midnight. This time, she wasn't standing there. I waited for her and then drove around aimlessly for a while, but she didn't turn up. *She should have come.*

I hadn't told her I would return, but so what? She should have understood. I had been so anxious to see her – how could she not feel the same way?

I could still feel the sensation of her soft, red lips.

I gently wet my lips with my tongue. I wanted her! Wanted her desperately! Now, right now!

I turned and drove towards the studio. The place was lit up, which meant that shooting was still in progress. I could understand the reason for her delay the moment I stepped into the studio.

I turned towards the set, moving through a crowd of onlookers. The set seemed to be of some third-rate Hindi movie, but was massive. There was even a white and gold chariot.

I asked the person standing next to me, 'What scene is this?'

The dishevelled man said, excitedly, 'Don't you know? *Dracula.* We're making *Dracula* in Hindi,' as if he was the producer.

Now things started making sense to me. That must be Dracula's ride!

'But, Dracula's carriage is always black in the Hollywood films,' I said.

The shabby man answered, 'This is not his! A female vampire is to arrive in this and kiss the hero. A blood-sucking kiss!'

I laughed aloud. 'That's so strange. How are you going to show kissing in a Hindi movie?'

'Oh! No problem. We'll shoot it from the back!' he said with a sneer.

Suddenly, everything fell silent and the clap sounded. The filming had begun.

The set was bathed in bright lights and the jungles in the background came to life.

The camera slowly began moving forward. She stood in the middle, facing the other way. She was clad in a white sari and her hair was loose. The hero stood next to her. He had long hair and was handsome. The next moment, he held her in a tight embrace. Her back was still to the camera. She left him in a moment and his body slumped to the ground in a heap.

Then she went and sat in the chariot. The director shouted, 'Cut!'

The silence broke and there was a ruckus all around.

I moved away from the crowd and walked towards her. I held her by the shoulder and turned her towards me.

I was stunned. It was someone else!

She looked just like her from behind. Exactly like her! But their faces were totally different.

'What do you want?' she asked in a throaty voice.

I explained to her in brief and gave her the address.

'Oh! That one?' the girl said. 'She didn't come today. She left without completing the scene yesterday. Only a few shots were left and so they used me as her double.'

'Why didn't she come today? Any message?' I asked.

'Yes, there was a message this afternoon,' the girl said. 'She died this morning.'

I walked to my car, parked outside the studio. Everything was silent. There was a dull moon in the sky. I accelerated and the road seemed to disappear from under me.

Suddenly, I felt a gentle tap on my shoulder.

I stopped the car.

She was sleeping on the back seat, but her hand kept moving on my shoulder.

I opened the door and stepped out. I opened the back door and there she was: lying happily with a broad smile.

She looked divine in the mild moonlight. There was a mystical glow on her face and her red lips glistened like fresh blood.

I bent down.

She opened her eyes and gently began caressing my hair.

I bent closer to her dainty neck and placed my lips exactly where I had pierced her with my fangs last night.

My black car was bathed in moonlight.

WORMS

Damn it!

The sky was a brilliant saffron – until clouds gathered, thick and dark, threatening to burst. Just what I needed while driving through the hills over uneven terrain and close to steep drops. One wrong turn could be fatal.

Moreover, the car was new. Until recently, I had been driving the family car because Grandpa refused to buy me a new one. 'You're still too young,' he would say.

Finally, a few days ago – on my twenty-third birthday – I put my foot down. Grandpa relented and bought me the car. Of course, he did deliver quite the lecture: 'Look, you're the only son. In five years or so, I will not be able to do much. You will not be able to manage and all this will be a mess. Please learn to do things while I'm still alive and well.'

'Okay, Grandpa,' I said. 'I'll be responsible, but first, let's talk about the car. You know how I am. I want what I want.'

He bought me the Chevrolet, but not without more words of wisdom: 'Look here, you will be able to drive your new car only because you had been driving mine all these days. It's the same principle for landownership too. You need to learn, otherwise it will be very difficult to manage all this property. The tribals in this area are a troublesome lot. You need to understand them well. Driving around and relaxing will not help. We have protected this land for generations. We have developed it acre by acre. You need to take care of it and expand it. If you fail to gain from it, all will be lost. It will become a tax burden and you may need to sell it off at a ridiculous price. You will be left with empty coffers!'

I was just happy to have a car of my own, which I fell in love with at first sight. If I were to drive it in Delhi, I'd be lost in a swarm of college beauties just dying to join me for a ride. There were so many adventures to be had with my gorgeous Chevy, but driving it in the hills was not something I had been looking forward to. Nervous, I stayed under thirty kilometres per hour.

Should I try going faster? It would be nice to be home soon.

When the impending rain did eventually pour, it became difficult to see, even with the headlights on. Everything was a blur and it was hard to tell the hills from the clouds.

Why on earth did Grandpa choose to buy land here, of all places? No one in these parts could appreciate nice clothes or a cool car – they only greeted us because we were landlords. Pitiful!

The foremen were really stupid, so what could one say about the people working under them? It's a sorry sight, watching them toil on land they don't own, repaying debts with sweat and blood. They were like earthworms. Yes, just like worms, they were completely uncultured and such eyesores to boot! It was painful to look at their emaciated bodies and sunken eyes.

The women were different though, and very attractive: dark, strong and sturdy! A refreshing change from the prissy Delhi girls. The ones working on the land were so damn sexy that a man could harden at the very sight of them. It helped that they were so scantily clad – thin saris with no blouses. It was difficult not to stare.

Rainwater flowed down the road, and the ground grew slushy under the wheels. The car could easily get stuck in the mud. *Oh baby, what is destined for you today?*

I was almost crawling up the road when I stopped the car and wondered what to do next. Should I go ahead or stop for some time? Was there a house anywhere nearby where I could take shelter? I pulled out the flask of whiskey from my pocket, and downed a neat peg. The kick from the mahua liquor I had enjoyed at the farm had begun to ebb, and this was the perfect solution to a dull drive. I wondered if it was okay to mix whiskey and mahua.

The sky grew darker, but the rain would not subside and drummed the roof of the car. I decided to stop at the first house I saw as my eyelids began to get heavy. *Shit! You can never be sure with these local drinks!*

I spotted a lamp flickering in the distance and drove up to it. There was no house, just two small huts, with smooth mud walls. One of them had a light in the window.

I took another swig and stepped out of the car. The sound of the car door alerted one of the residents, who emerged from the hut. It was difficult to see the stranger, who was silhouetted by the light of the lamp.

She must have recognized me as the landlord's son. After all, I had been at the farm earlier and, besides, who else owns a car in these parts? I rushed into the hut to escape the rain and she followed me in.

Once inside, I could see her clearly. Wow! I had never seen a body like that before: skin glistening like bronze, a perfectly placed nose, high cheekbones, big black eyes and moist, pouting lips! She wore a yellow cloth around her waist, but nothing to cover her full breasts.

I was overcome with lust, and couldn't care less for what she was trying to say. I pulled off the cloth and pushed her to the ground, holding her down as she tried to push me away.

I tried to kiss her lips, but she turned her face away. Soon, everything became hazy. Her struggling got weaker and my intoxication reached its peak. I could only feel the rub of her naked body against my clothes and the increasing hardness between my legs.

Finally I slowed down and everything went still. She lay motionless as I rested my head on her breasts.

Suddenly, I felt strange. Someone else was in the room. I got up with a start, snapping out of my dazed state. He stood there, still.

His eyes glistened in the darkness. Like fire.

He didn't say a word to me. Did not approach.

Bloody worm! He recognized me. I was his master and he a labourer in my farm. He dare not touch me! If I chose to spare him, it was my prerogative – and more than enough to compensate her. After all, I had my self-respect and sense of empathy. I put my hand in my pocket and pulled out whatever money I had, before placing it near her. It was a twenty-rupee note.

He didn't move to retrieve it. He just stood there, staring at me with those flaming eyes. He was dark and thin and was wearing a dirty cloth around his waist, like all the other men.

Unlike the other men, he did not wear a defeated expression on his face. Of course, it may have appeared so because of those blazing eyes.

I placed a five-rupee note with the twenty. He walked out without touching the money.

I walked out and turned around to see her sitting in the hut with her head buried between her knees.

He said nothing as he stared at my car.

Bloody worm! That's all you and your kind are. What can you do by staring at the car! You will never even sit in one. I started the car without looking at him, satisfied that the twenty-five rupees had been worth it. She was so exotic and different from the skinny, fair ones I was used to. I wondered if I should have her brought to the bungalow sometime. After all, that pest couldn't do anything for her. He couldn't even buy her clothes. The moment I thought about clothing, my mind went back to her wide, smooth thighs. I realized then that one of the reasons she had been so much fun was because she had resisted, unlike the willing Delhi girls. Forcing myself upon her had given me a thrill.

What had she got to lose anyway? They wouldn't have seen twenty-five rupees in their lives. When do they ever get so much money at one time? They labour on the fields all day. He would go crazy with happiness seeing that sum of money! I wouldn't be surprised if he asked me to come over daily. What morals did those worms have anyway—

Suddenly, the car came to a halt. It didn't move an inch and I would need to step out of the car to see about the problem.

The rain picked up yet again. I got out and opened the bonnet. Everything was in perfect condition. Puzzled, I shut the bonnet.

I got back in and tried to start the car again. It didn't work. *Damn this car! Damn this rain! Damn everything! Damn! Damn!*

With my head against the steering wheel, I tried to think of a solution. What could have gone wrong? I decided to let a mechanic take a look at it, but that could only happen the next day.

But what about the present? How would I go home?

It was late in the night and there was no sign of the rain stopping.

I was tired and contemplated finding a place to rest. Grandpa would worry, but that was a problem for later. Suddenly, a thought crossed my mind. There were just a couple of huts there. There should have been a settlement. Why was the man living there, all alone? Was there something special about him?

Again, the car refused to start and I wondered if it was a bad omen, if the man had cursed it. I chided myself for being superstitious, but I couldn't forget his flaming eyes.

I lifted my head off the wheel and was paralyzed by the fear of what I saw.

Those two fiery eyes were staring at me through the darkness.

My heart began pounding. I took a swig from the flask, hoping it was just my mind playing tricks on me.

But no, they were still there.

I stuck my head out of the window and shouted, 'Who's there?'

He approached. It was the man from the hut. He moved closer and stood near the car, drenched.

I opened the door and stepped out. He stretched out his hand with the two soiled, dirty notes.

I quietly took them from him and put them back in my pocket. He started walking back, only turning once with a nod.

I locked the car and followed him. The rain stopped suddenly. I couldn't see much in the darkness, but he moved briskly, aware that I was behind him.

A loud moan echoed through the valley. I got gooseflesh but reminded myself that it was probably a wolf howl. But it did not stop.

Soon we reached his hut and went in. He asked me if I would like to eat some bhakhris.

I refused. I was too tired, but there was not enough room for the three of us in the hut. I wondered if she would even sleep if I were in the same space.

It was a miracle that, despite what had happened earlier, the man could empathize with me and invite me back. But how did he know I would get stuck? He must have realized it when he came to return the money. Still, it was odd that he knew he could catch up with me.

I was too exhausted to think about it and the sleeping arrangements seemed more important. Then, I remembered the second hut. The one with no light in the window.

He walked over to the next one with a small lamp and opened the door. There was grass spread on the floor.

He finally asked, 'Will you be able to sleep here?'

'Of course.'

'No, I asked because my pets are here.'

'Where? I can't see them. What kind of pets do you have?'

'Worms,' he said.

I felt like laughing. Great! What other pet could he have?

When I agreed to stay on, he closed the door and left. I lay down on the grass in peace. Worms! I felt like laughing again. What could they do besides wriggle in the mud, ready to be crushed?

I did eventually fall asleep but, suddenly, I woke up to some movement in the grass. I pulled out the lighter and lit the lamp. I looked around but couldn't see anything. Then, I spotted it in a corner of the hut. A black snake raised its head from the grass. I placed the lamp on the floor and ran towards the door. There was a yellow snake near the entrance – blocking my path.

I looked around for an escape and screamed. There were about ten or fifteen different types of snakes in that little hut and they were all moving towards me.

He called them worms! The bloody fool! These snakes could kill a man in an instant!

I was sure my presence had woken them up, but in the next instant, I wondered if I was hallucinating. Perhaps they were worms and I was seeing things. Yes, they might just be worms.

No. They were real. It was not a hallucination. They were not worms. They were snakes. And they were closing in.

Save me! Someone, please save me!

Even as I shuddered with fear, I wondered: Why? Why did he call them worms?

A HOUSE OF MY OWN

This is the story of how I got my house.

I should introduce myself before I go on, shouldn't I? I'm Madhu Sane, the last of the Sanes – a line with little else but me to their name. Of course, there were benefits that came with being an orphan: I did not have the responsibility of managing a house and there was no one to tell me what to do, or to interrupt me while I worked. I was single and free. I could visit the gymnasium twice a day, once in the morning and again in the evening. I had school in the afternoon. I would manage to pass each year. I had a few friends and no problems with anyone in town. All in all, days passed by quite smoothly.

Except certain days, when I did feel something was amiss. Days when I longed for a house of my own. I longed for a place to stay in that wasn't a temple or an ashram – a place to call home, where I could eat in peace and exchange a few words of love with someone.

I would then tell myself that I would complete my matriculation, go into the city to search for a job, and study further. Even if it did cost me a lot, I would rent a two-room house. I would get married and have a proper household. Then no one would dare call me an orphan, or helpless or homeless.

But that was many years away.

Sada Chikhalikar's situation was very different from mine. We were a gang of six boys. I was the youngest at seventeen. The others had spent a year or two in a few classes and were older than me. I was on scholarship and could not afford to fail, but I was always jealous of Sada. No one in our gang liked him. He was a moneylender's son and a pampered one at that. He would demand things like an entitled brat. No one ever denied him his wishes. To make things worse, he wasn't kind either. Despite getting what he wanted, he would throw tantrums. He had servants at his beck and call. They ruled over the village. That was the only reason we had allowed him to stay in our gang. After all, making enemies with him was akin to making enemies with the moneylender. And that meant making enemies with the whole village. I did not care. But then, I used to eat in four different houses. I could not afford to have them shut their doors on me. It was no surprise that no one ever came in Sada Chikhalikar's way. We were forced to tolerate his eccentricities, his bullying and his foul language.

But one day, he crossed all limits. It was not an unusual situation. Something which happened often enough. When I look back, I'm surprised by how it escalated. We had a boy called Gampu in our gang. He was a mild-mannered guy. His sister had gone into the woods to pluck some berries and it was getting dark. Suddenly, Sada appeared and tried to grab her, pulling at her dupatta. The poor girl started screaming. Luckily, a few of us were nearby and we rushed to the spot. I tackled Sada to the ground and beat him hard. My blows were relentless – I wanted to teach him a lesson for life.

The next day we met at school. All of us behaved as if nothing had happened the previous evening. We all spoke with Sada normally. He was a little cautious in the beginning, but warmed up later.

A week after that episode, Sada approached me after school and said, 'Scholar! (He was the only one who addressed me so.) Let's go to Jahangir's haveli today.'

It was a common belief that the haveli was haunted. Located far away from the boundaries of the village, we weren't sure why it was called Jahangir's haveli. Apparently, the owner was a businessman living in Bombay, but no one had ever seen him, and no one knew a thing about his business.

The haveli was old and almost crumbling. No one other than a watchman lived there, but people had seen a lamp burning inside it. People spoke of seeing a figure roaming its halls at around midnight. The figure looked like an old woman. Some also spoke of having heard the sound of her walking stick tapping on the floor. Others claimed to have seen a young girl on the grounds, and it was said that she had four eyes.

The watchman claimed that some of the old utensils had vanished over time. In fact, the watchman himself was a strange sort of character. He barely spoke and was reticent even if you tried to strike up a conversation.

Our gang was fascinated by the haveli. We would speculate about it being haunted. We had even placed a bet and often made plans to go and find out for ourselves. But the plans never materialized. After all, no one wanted to be the first to find out if the rumours were true.

I was thus surprised and curious when Sada spoke of going to the old place. I asked, 'Why? Do you want to see the ghost?'

'Come on! What ghosts?' Sada said. 'People talk a lot. We should go and solve the mystery for ourselves.'

'Fine with me. I'm ready. Should we go at midnight?'

'No, no! Not at midnight. My folks won't allow it. We'll go after sunset so we can be back before dinner.'

'Done! Let the others know.'

'No! Let's not involve them. I don't want another argument. And if something really turns up there, I don't want them shitting themselves. The two of us will go. We can always take them later.'

I agreed. The gang would create a racket. Besides, it would be more of a thrill if it was just the two of us. I waited anxiously for sunset, and when it was finally time to go, I met up with Sada by the stream.

◆

He walked with his hands in his pockets and I asked, 'What are you carrying in there?' He merely smiled in reply. The sudden call of a lapwing made us jump out of our skins. We laughed at our own nervousness. Here we were – waiting to find out if the haveli was haunted while being startled by a bird.

It was soon dark. We approached the haveli and climbed over its boundary wall. That was when a knife fell out of Sada's pocket. He quickly picked it up. 'Well, you need this in such places. Always helps!'

I did not react. I had not asked him for an explanation.

We met the frail, old watchman near the main gate. He held up a lamp that cast its dull glow over half his face. And his eyes – I had never seen such eyes in my life. There was fear in them. He stared at us for a moment and a shiver ran down my spine. Finally, he locked the gate and walked away without saying a word.

We jumped over the gate and landed on the grounds, wondering why he had even bothered with the lock.

The handle of the main door was rusty and we struggled a little before getting it to creak open. There was a layer of dust over everything inside. The huge drawing room was empty except for a few paintings, a worn chair, a few broken stools and similar items.

We walked towards the door at the far end. Sada stayed behind me, maybe out of fear. I pulled him forward and we opened the door together. There was a single bed in the room, with a filthy, ruined mattress. I moved the torch around to check the room when Sada said, pointing in one direction, 'Look there, in the upper corner.'

I aimed my torch there and squinted to figure out what we were looking at. All we could see were spider webs. Before I could turn towards Sada, I felt a sharp pain tear through my ribs. For a moment I could not breathe. The pain got worse, and darkness thickened around my vision until everything faded.

Black.

I felt light, relieved. I was free. The pain was gone. I could float, go wherever I wished. I felt I could fit into the tiniest of places. I went to the window and saw the grounds clearly bathed in moonlight. Then I saw him in the distance – holding a blood-stained knife. Sada was running away. Escaping.

I then realized what had happened. Sada had taken his revenge. The thought left me weak. A light wind blew as I dozed off by the window.

I woke up the next morning. Or, rather, I felt awake. It was not like waking up from sleep, but more like lucid sleepwalking. Everything looked unreal. I – my consciousness – was floating in the air. What was that on the bed, I wondered.

Oh my god! It was my own body. I could see three wounds where the knife had been plunged in my back. The blood had dried to a dark brown.

I wanted to wail, rant, scream. But there was no way to vent my rage. I saw my hopes and dreams and ambitions flash by: a good job, a wife, a house. My house ... my very own house...

I composed myself, eventually, and soon started thinking differently. I wondered if the watchman would notice the body lying in the room. It was unlikely. The room looked like it had not been swept or cleaned in ages. Then it hit me – the haveli was supposed to be haunted, and now, I could find out if that was true.

I floated through all the rooms. I did not see anything other than a thick layer of dust and some odd furniture. I was tempted to trace my name in the dust, but could not form fingers.

I floated back to my body and hovered around it. With effort, I focussed my will to wipe the froth from my mouth – and it gave me an idea. I could squeeze myself back into my body through the mouth. I tried it and was amazed – I was in. My body started stirring. I lifted my neck and stood up. I could move.

It was not as easy as before and felt like I was wearing ill-fitting clothes. Still, it was better than nothing. I needed the body until I was comfortable moving around. At that moment, I saw a shadow outside, in the veranda.

It was a girl, about the same age as me. She was at the door and stopped in her tracks after noticing me. No words escaped my mouth. She turned to run, but looked back in time to see me gesture for her to stop. She waited and I tried to walk towards her, even though I could not move fast. After struggling to get close, I waved her over. She approached.

'Have you seen my grandmother?' she asked me. I shook my head. In fact, I barely paid attention to what she was saying. I was too distracted by her face and the extra set of eyebrows. I wondered if she was the ghost girl from the rumours.

'What are you staring at? My eyebrows?' she asked.

I nodded.

'I hurt my forehead when I was younger. It left a scar.'

'Oh,' I said, realizing I had found my voice. It sounded weird, as if coming from deep within a well. It was the sound of a person in fear.

I suppose she too was taken aback hearing me. But I quickly corrected the situation by tapping my throat with my fingers to suggest it was sore. She smiled and started walking away when I said, 'Was your grandmother here?'

She stopped dead in her tracks. Realizing that it was not right to talk there, in the open, we stepped inside. Then she was unstoppable. Clearly, she had no one else to talk to, but much to say.

She said she lived with her grandmother in a hut nearby. Her grandmother would, avoiding the watchman's eyes, steal things from the haveli. Despite the girl's protests, the old woman continued stealing. The girl had come looking for her grandmother.

That explained everything: the apparition of the old woman, the ghost girl and the missing objects. I felt foolish about losing my life trying to figure out if the place had been haunted.

She went on, 'People say this place is haunted.' She laughed. 'Tchah! There are no ghosts here. People are simply scared for no reason. You know, I too was scared for a moment when I saw you. But does that mean...' She shook her head. It was a good thing she hadn't seen the wounds on my back.

I saw her grandmother that night, but she could not see me. I had left my body, having grown tired of dragging it around, but had ensured that it was well hidden.

The old woman entered with a lamp, pottered around for a while, and then started walking away with something in her hand. To have some fun, I blew out her lamp. I was hoping she would get scared but all she mumbled was, 'Damn wind!' I wanted to scare her, but if she were to fall ill her granddaughter would be burdened unnecessarily. To tell the truth, I liked that girl. Her sweet voice, the way she talked, and her casual manner was attractive.

Three or four days passed. My initial belief that there was no one in the haveli other than me turned out to be right. I was getting used to floating around without my body. One evening, I stood in front of the old watchman who was lighting a beedi. I blew out the flame. Quite naturally, he could not see me. He struck another match and, once again, I extinguished it. This happened three or four times. Next, I sat on his shoulders making him jump out of his skin. I broke a small twig and waved it in the air in front of him. He stared at the twig with widening eyes before running away. I was sure he wouldn't return after that fright.

Soon, my body started to rot – the body I had trained in the gym, scrubbed clean in the river, treated for wounds and illnesses. All that effort had ended with me watching it decompose in an abandoned, old haveli. I couldn't bring myself to look at the discoloured skin and the eyes that were fixed in a vacant stare. I couldn't let the girl see it, but how would I meet her without a body?

I entered my decomposing former shell and managed to stagger to Chikhalikar's house on a bright, full-moon night. I saw Sada walk out, but he ignored me. 'Sada!' I called, but he did not turn. I hobbled behind him and called out once more. Finally, he turned – just in time to catch my hideous grin. That one look was enough to send his eyes rolling back as he fell unconscious. For a moment I was tempted to put my freezing hand to his neck. He would have died instantly. I took a step forward but then realization dawned on me. If he were to die, he too would be like me. He might even demand to stay in the haveli with me. That would lead to fights, arguments and mental anguish.

I turned back, leaving Sada on the ground. I was going to prove that I was smarter than him, and not a victim overcome by his thirst for vengeance. Besides, I would have my revenge the way it was meant to be enjoyed – cold. And I had enough time for that.

A few days later, I went back to Sada but without my body. He was sleeping. I sat on his chest and pounded him with my fists. He squirmed in agony. I then took the lit candle from the side table and pushed it up his nose. His screams woke up the entire house. I knew that if I continued this long enough, Sada would go mad. That is what I wanted. I did not want him to die. I wanted the moneylender's son to go mad and roam the streets in tatters. I knew that Sada's greedy brothers would throw him out of their home the day their father died. Yes, I would see to it that he was shunned by society and thrown out of his house.

When my body decayed considerably, I put it in a small, dark room, surrendering it to rats and other scavengers, along with my happiness and sorrows and dreams. Finally, I felt truly free.

I could float in any corner of the haveli. Sometimes, I floated out of the window and perched on the tamarind tree, listening to the hooting of the owls, the flapping of the bats. It was entertaining but I did feel lonely and missed having someone's company at times. On evening, when I felt desperately lonely, I decided I had to kill the girl with the eyebrow scars. That way, she could join me and we could enjoy eternity together. Besides, she wouldn't miss the world of the living, with its pain and poverty. With her, I was sure I could find happiness.

And I was right. In the end I got what I wanted: a wife and a house. A house of my own.

PRAYER

'Shh…' I said. 'Speak softly. The staff might think we're fighting.'

'Let them,' Kimbahune barked. 'Tell me, why don't you make P. Ratilal understand? If he can't keep the balance books updated he might as well close the company. You and that Upadhyay are too soft.'

Having walked in without knocking, Ms Shivare had heard him.

'Shivare!' Kimbahune shouted, directing his anger at him. 'You are supposed to knock before entering. How many times am I supposed to remind you? Can't you follow some basic discipline? How many years have you been working here?'

Shivare did not speak. She did not even try to apologize, making Kimbuhane even angrier.

'Shivare, say sorry,' he shouted.

She mumbled the word without emotion.

'Now get out. Come back after ten minutes. I'm in the middle of an important discussion. And don't forget to knock next time.'

Shivare threw a glance at me before leaving. The look in her eyes carried many meanings.

Instead of wasting five minutes insulting Shivare, Kimbahune could have just asked her what she wanted. But he was not known to possess such wisdom.

That evening, when the staff was leaving and I was alone, Shivare walked over to me. I asked, a little surprised, 'How come you haven't left yet?'

'I'm not in a hurry,' she said. 'There's no one waiting for me back home.'

I did not know that she lived alone, but didn't probe further.

'I did not like the way Kimbuhane Sahib shouted at you. Frankly, you are far more efficient than him. You should be in his place. He does not deserve to be here.'

'Leave it, Shivare. It takes all kinds of people to make this world,' I said, changing the topic. I wasn't about to start gossiping about my boss with a subordinate. It was inappropriate.

'People like Kimbahune don't deserve to live in this world.' She said it without any anger, but there was a sense of finality in her tone.

I looked at her sharply and she left without saying another word.

I observed her for some time. She had stayed late in the office as there was no one waiting for her back home. Likewise, there was no one to accompany her home. Was she hoping I would give her company? Had she come with the expectation that I would ask her to stay? So that I may go with her? But I did not stop her or offer her my company. Like most other people, I too sensed a certain coldness while interacting with her. It was not easy to point out the reason for it, but she did not seem like one of us. There was something impervious about her, something impenetrable. She was no different otherwise. She had a reasonably good-looking face, with pleasant features. She was dusky and taller than the average woman. Her voice was husky and she stood out in the crowd because of her height, her slim figure, her hair left loose and the way she wore a bright sari and a matching blouse. But instead of being attracted to her, people maintained a certain distance from her. Perhaps it was the cool and measured tone she spoke with. It was natural that someone like Kimbahune was irritated with her.

There was increasing friction between Kimbahune and Shivare. He would shout at her even in the presence of staff, and over trivial matters like the filing of documents, and would scream at her when she neglected to hand over files on time. He ranted and said all kinds of things to her, but she barely spoke a sentence. Her silence was cold and sharp, and her eyes piercing.

Every time he asked her to say sorry, she merely parroted the word in an icy monotone. People in her place would have cried, overwhelmed with shame and anger. But she did nothing of that sort, making Kimbahune angrier. He would say things that were uncalled for and she would stand and listen, as if simply taking note of his behaviour.

I was present during one such episode. After he had calmed down, I said to Kimbahune, 'Sir, please don't mind, but can't you be a little more lenient with Shivare?'

'Am I abusing her physically? Slapping her or hitting her?'

'No, I didn't mean that. But, you know, scolding her unnecessarily and that too in the presence of everyone...'

'What do you mean in the presence of everyone? Is it a romance to be conducted privately? In matters of discipline, it is better to set an example.'

'I agree. But she, being a woman, I just feel that ... we must show some restraint...'

'That thick-skinned bitch did not even shed a tear. She kept staring at me shamelessly. Forget it! Why do you want to take her side in all this? Is there some affection there?'

There was no point explaining anything to him. I gave up.

Two days later, I was sitting in the office in the late evening after most of the staff had left. I was about to enter Kimbahune's office to discuss a problem regarding a charitable trust when I heard him shout 'Get out!' at someone. Within a few minutes, Shivare stepped out. She would always stop to acknowledge me, but this time she completely ignored me. She walked away, lost in thought.

I knocked at his door and, though I did not hear a 'yes', I walked in.

Kimbahune sat with his head in his hands, as if he had suffered a huge shock.

'Sir, what is it?' I asked.

'Bloody bitch!' he mumbled to himself.

'What happened, sir?'

He came to his senses after a while, drank some water and went to the attached bathroom. When he returned, he lowered himself into his chair and said, 'She said I would die soon.'

'What?'

'Yes. She said I was going to die ... within a few days.'

'I don't get it. Start from the beginning.'

He explained, but I couldn't believe what I was hearing.

A few minutes earlier, Shivare had entered Kimbahune's cabin after asking for permission. She was wearing a red sari with a black border and a matching black blouse. Her hair, as always, was kept loose. She was dressed normally, but somehow Kimbahune felt unsettled. Afraid. There was something about her eyes.

She sat down before he could ask her to.

He asked, 'What is it?'

'Sir, I have come to tell you,' she began quietly, 'that you are not fit to live in this world any longer.'

'Get out!' Kimbahune shouted.

She said, without a trace of emotion, 'That is why you will die. Very soon.'

Kimbahune could not utter a word after that.

'I'm going to start a prayer from today. For you to die. I will be praying with all my heart. And I am sure that my prayers will be heard. But before starting such prayers, it is a custom to inform the person who is going to die. Hence, I am informing you. I am starting the prayers...' she said in a tone so cold that it could have cut through one's heart. She then stood up and walked out of the cabin.

I was shocked. I would not have believed him, but I had seen her walk out of his cabin in a trance. I was, in some sense, a witness.

'That bitch! How dare she come into my cabin and tell me that to my face.'

'Maybe she just made a bet with someone,' I tried to make light of the situation. 'I'm sure she will come and apologize.'

'I definitely expect her to. Or I will sack her. Look at her temerity. That whore!'

'She must be wanting to see how angry you can get. Anyway, the whole thing is nothing more than a practical joke. I had come here to discuss the Dharamshala charitable trust. You had...'

'Leave aside the trust for a while,' he said. 'Tell me, are you aware of such practices? I mean, can someone pray for another's death?'

'Not at all! There is no reason to get so upset. She's a little odd. She does what comes to her mind. You know that. She's a fool!'

'That may be ... but her insanity is going to cost her. I will issue a notice tomorrow itself. What does she think of herself? She won't get away with this!' Kimbahune shouted. I noticed that his voice lacked the usual anger. It seemed like he was trying to act angry.

Kimbahune spoke of issuing a termination notice but I sensed that he was deeply afraid. Not only did he not discuss the issue of the charitable trust, he even left earlier than usual. He asked me to join him in his car saying, 'Let's chat!' While chatting casually, he did suggest that I try to find out what Shivare had in mind.

I was not planning to fall for the suggestion. Asking her about the incident would give it attention it did not deserve. Besides, I had never spoken to her of my own accord. No one spoke to her much. And if I did, it would be noticed by others. And I could not afford to spoil my image.

But I did keep an eye on her. I noticed that she would, in her spare time or during lunchtime, mumble something softly. She had the same look on her face as she had when she walked out of Kimbahune's cabin the other day. People had started gossiping.

I did not take the issue seriously. Her mumbling, her trance – I ignored it all as part of her insanity. But I decided to meet my psychiatrist friend, Devras.

'Devras,' I asked, 'can one pray for another's death?'

'Why not?' he asked back. 'We pray for others' success, victory and health. We pray for their long life, don't we? Then why can we not pray for someone to die?'

I had never thought along those lines. I was confused. I said, 'Don't we ask for good things when we pray? We don't ask for bad things to happen.'

'Who can decide what is truly good or bad? A bad man dying may be good for others. The success of an evil man can be dangerous for society. We have different gods. Who shall we pray to? The power which gives us strength can also be evil.'

I shivered involuntarily. I wondered who Shivare prayed to.

'Leave aside gods and demons for a moment. I will tell you from a purely psychological point of view,' Devras said. 'I am talking of faith. Conviction. If a man is convinced that he is destined to die, nothing can save him. No prayer, chant, black magic ... nothing!'

'I don't understand.'

'There is such a black magic. It exists in different cultures. The target usually starts getting weaker when he is shunned by others and told his days are numbered. He becomes paranoid and starts wasting away. If someone is unaware that he is the target, nothing is likely to happen to him. It is their faith in their impending doom that kills them.'

I decided to tell Kimbahune about it. I disliked him, but I had to fulfil my duty.

The very next day I met him and asked, 'You were planning to give notice to Shivare? What happened?'

'I decided not to.'

'That's great! I feel she needs the job.'

'Upadhyay, you are always taking her side. I think you are attracted to her. But let me make it clear: I haven't changed my mind because she needs the job.'

'Then?'

'I feel she might get further agitated if I issue the notice. I mean, she mentioned her prayer yesterday. I don't believe in it, but why rake the issue further?'

That meant Kimbahune was worried. He was scared.

'Sir, what can she do in any case?'

Kimbahune's face turned serious. He said, 'I was not planning to tell you ... but I saw her last night!'

'Where? In your dreams?' I tried joking.

'No. In the playground in front of my house. It was around ten at night. I was standing in the balcony enjoying a drink when I saw her. She was sitting on the ground, her hands folded in prayer. She was staring at my house!'

'I don't believe that! She was at the playground at night – what for?'

'She was praying. For my death.'

'What did you do?'

'I had half a mind to call the police. To say that I could see some suspicious woman in the ground near my house. I thought she deserved to spend a night behind bars! But I didn't want to aggravate the issue. I just called out her name. She simply stood up and walked away, staring at my house as she went.'

'Can I say something? Just banish these thoughts. No one dies just because someone else wishes it.'

'I don't believe in such nonsense either. Even if ten people were to pray for my death, nothing would happen to me.'

'That's the spirit!'

'Nevertheless, I think you can convince her to stop all this. Can't you?'

'Well, let me think about it. Don't worry, sir.'

That evening I was looking for a book on marketing law when I saw her sitting at her desk. Silently sitting, looking down. Her hands were folded on the desk.

I approached her, but she seemed to be in a trance. I noticed that she had a photograph of Kimbahune on the table. It was from our office magazine. She was staring at the photo and mumbling something softly.

I said, 'Shivare, what is all this?'

She said, without bothering to hide the photo, 'Prayers.'

'Prayers? For what?'

She did not answer.

I asked, 'Shivare, last night ... were you sitting in the playground opposite Kimbahune's house?'

I knew what she would say: '*Why should I go there? He might have imagined it...*'

But she did not say any of that. She replied, putting the photo in her bag, 'Yes.'

I was dumbstruck. I asked, 'What were you doing there?'

'Praying.'

'For Kimbahune to die?'

'Yes.'

'Why?'

'I told you the other day. Such a person should not exist in the world.'

'Maybe. But people don't die just because someone prays for it.'

'They do.'

'How? It's impossible.'

'Wait for it. You'll see for yourself.' She picked up her purse and walked away with a straight back.

Well, Kimbahune was surely getting weaker by the day. Not only had he stopped scolding Shivare, he would even avoid meeting her. He had stopped his screaming and shouting and abusing. Everyone noticed the change and wondered why it had come about.

Shivare meanwhile had started ignoring her work. Not that she was making mistakes, but she had started palming off her work to others. She soon had a lot of free time, which she would use to stare blankly or look at the photograph while chanting softly.

People made fun of her, made snide remarks and gossiped amongst themselves, but she continued to ignore them. She behaved as if she was unaware of people around her. She would use even five minutes of free time for her chants. After a while, people started paying closer attention to her activities and were soon scared. Most tried to avoid her.

'Upadhyay, there is nothing to worry about,' Kimbahune said.

'What do you mean?' I asked.

'I mean ... my health! Absolutely perfect. Everything is normal. I got the reports just yesterday. The doctor said I am perfectly fit.'

He was worried enough to see a doctor. So much for all that bravado.

The very next day, when I had reached home and barely changed my clothes, I got a phone call. 'Come to Nanavati right away. Kimbahune has been admitted. He was in a car accident.'

I reached the hospital immediately. A jeep had rammed into his car. He was in the driver's seat and his face had been smashed into the windscreen. The steering wheel had penetrated his chest, damaging his lungs. It was impossible for him to survive.

He died within an hour of my reaching the hospital.

There was chaos in the office the next morning. No one was at their desk. They were all huddled in small groups, discussing Kimbahune's death. I had to use my authority to get some order.

After a lot of phone calls with the head office, I was told that I was to take over temporarily in place of Kimbahune. Finally, we got back to work and held a prayer meeting as per protocol.

Shivare sat up front during the prayer meeting. Right opposite me. She constantly stared at me. Most people had come to know of Kimbahune's death only after reaching the office. But she knew it already – she was even dressed in a white sari and was no longer in a trance. She looked triumphant.

It was not a victory for her. Kimbahune had died in an accident. How was it related to her? But she walked around the office the whole day with a light step. She was no longer praying and chanting. In fact, she was more talkative than usual. The people in the office too felt relaxed and were not scared of her. She did not stay back that evening and left with the rest of the crowd.

I had a lot of work and it was nearly nine when I finished. I stretched myself, twisted and turned my back, and left feeling a little relaxed.

I did not go home, but arrived at Devras's house.

He had just returned from his clinic. We chatted over drinks.

I asked, after describing the events, 'So, do you think Shivare's prayers were answered?'

'I cannot say that with certainty, but I think she did succeed.'

'How can you say that? What, according to you as a psychiatrist, was the objective of the prayers? To create a disturbance in Kimbahune's mind? To make him believe that he was going to die?'

'Absolutely right.'

'Where is the question of mind here? He died in an accident.'

Devras smiled. He said, 'How do you know he wasn't distracted by the thought of death? A distraction that took his life in the form of an accident? Perhaps he saw the jeep as the death he had been dreading.'

I could not counter that logic.

'Listen, in psychiatric language, this is called auto-suggestion: to follow and implement instructions given by the subconscious mind.' Devras laughed at the pun on the word 'auto.'

A letter arrived from the head office after a couple of days. I was being promoted in place of Kimbahune.

I shifted to his cabin, and that evening, as I was sitting alone and working, I heard a knock on the door. Soon, Shivare entered.

'Congratulations!' she said, smiling a little.

'Thank you!'

'It happened the way I wanted. You are sitting in Kimbahune's place.'

'Well this is what god wanted.'

'And my prayers helped. I prayed for his death!'

I tried laughing it off and said, 'Oh, come on! That was just a coincidence. Nothing more than that!'

'It is not a mere coincidence,' she said, staring. 'He died because of my prayers.'

I did not want to argue.

'I prayed for his death because he was a bad man. But I also wanted you to be in his place. You deserve to sit in this cabin. That was another reason. I killed Kimbahune for you.'

A shiver ran down my spine, but she seemed quite calm. She said, 'I did this for you. Only for you. I love you!'

Startled, I dropped a paperweight and it shattered against the floor.

She turned and left without another word. She was not bothered about my reaction. All she wanted was to let me know.

I kept looking at the door for a long time after she had left. Until the door stopped swinging.

I was in a shock. I knew she respected me and that she trusted me more than others. She was friendlier with me than with anyone else. But love?

I started looking at the situation from a different perspective. Did I not pay more attention to her than to other women? Had I not supported her when arguing with Kimbahune? Perhaps I did have feelings for her...

That was the problem. I was attracted to her. Or was it fear? Had she been like any other normal woman I would have accepted her love easily. But she had a strange power … a power she was proud of.

Bullshit! Since when did I believe in her powers?

Kimbahune's death was a mere coincidence. It was a simple accident. Or was it?

I spent a day and a night thinking of her. But I could not get any answers.

A full moon rose in the sky outside my window and my room was filled with moonlight.

I was in a beautiful dream: She was in my arms. She put her head on my chest and lay there. I was moving my fingers through her silken hair. I could not see her face, but I was sure it was beautiful.

I enjoyed the dream for a long time before opening my eyes to the moonlight.

And her! She was actually in my arms. I was moving my fingers through her hair.

I sat upright with a start, pushing her away.

'You … how did you get here?'

'What do you mean?' she chuckled. 'Not through the walls for sure. The front door was open. You were asleep. I didn't want to wake you.'

'I think you should go now,' I said, yet to recover from my shock. 'I don't want something to happen … something wrong.'

'What?' she said, seductively putting her hand around my neck. She muttered, pulling me closer, 'Whatever happens in this moonlight will be beautiful.'

I moved away, saying, 'Let me drop you home.'

'Why?' she asked, looking into my eyes. 'Don't you want me?'

'I don't want to be entangled with you. And banish any such thoughts from your head,' I said, a little harshly.

I might have been speaking to myself, and my voice was raised, trying to suppress my own objections to it.

She must have been surprised at my rude behaviour. She stared at me in disbelief. She said, 'How ungrateful you are! You don't care about what I did for you. You don't give a damn about my love. Listen! I am telling you: you will die. I will pray for it.'

She slammed the door behind her.

I sat on my bed, stunned. What was all this?

'Don't bother,' Devras said, trying to pacify me. 'You don't believe in this anyway. Why should you care?'

'It's not about whether I believe it or not. It's just strange when you think about it. Someone praying for my death.'

'I understand,' Devras said, taking on the role of a doctor. 'It's not that you are not interested in her. But you don't want to marry her as you are scared of her power. Am I right?'

'Absolutely!'

'But you don't believe in that power? You don't believe in the power of her prayers, right?'

'Right.'

'You must be sure, for if you do, you are dead! Such powers affect only the weak mind. Keep that thought alive. That is what will protect you.'

Two days later, I was standing at the window. The moonlight splashed over the garden. It was a lovely, starlit night.

I could see a huge peepal tree in the garden. The moonlight streamed through it, broken into fragments.

She sat there, in a trance. She sat staring at my window, unblinking.

I ran down and said, 'Come on, get up! Get out of here. I dare you to be seen anywhere near my house again.'

She stood up. She had a wicked smile on her face – one that would have frozen the blood of anyone looking at her.

'You can't scare me,' I said in a determined tone. 'You cannot do anything to me. I don't believe in any of your acts!'

I was out of breath having spoken to her. She stood there, staring at me.

Finally, I turned away and started climbing the stairs to my house.

Suddenly, I felt a slight ache in my chest.

Well, it had to be a coincidence … I didn't believe in her tricks.

The pain continued.

I decided to call my doctor the moment I was indoors.

I could hear her laughter, but I knew it was just my imagination. Yes, it had to be. The sound was just the rustling of peepal leaves.

I was not going to be scared any more. I could not let her win.

I got to my door, eager now to call the doctor. *Not that I believe. No, not at all.*

Still, I thought, it was better to call. After all, one can never be sure of what the future holds.

THE LOST CHILD

I answered the phone in the dim light of the lamp.

'Hello?'

'This is Dr Shirali from Shirali Clinic. Am I speaking to Sumit Sarang?'

'Yes.'

'*The* Sumit Sarang? The famous artist?'

'Yes,' I said, hoping he would spit it out.

'Is your son missing? Has he not returned home?'

'What?' I blurted, taken by surprise.

'A young boy has come over. Around ten years of age. I'll give you the details later, but he's asking for you.'

'This boy – is he alone or is there someone with him?'

'No. In fact, he's quite confused. We don't know what to do with him. We had no option but to call you.'

'I'm sorry, doctor,' I said, trying not to sound rude. 'I cannot help you. I don't have a son. I don't have any children!'

The doctor mumbled a sorry and disconnected.

'What happened?' Shreya asked in a sleepy voice.

'Nothing. Go back to sleep. Some doctor was asking if we were related to his patient. I told him we're not.'

Shreya turned and went back to sleep.

It would not make sense to explain everything to Shreya. I had to be careful of what I said to her, or risk reopening old wounds. I wish we could be satisfied with what we had, even if we didn't have children. After all, so many childless couples find happiness.

There was another reason for Shreya's sorrow. After a few years, when we went for a medical check-up, the doctor told her that it was her inability to conceive that kept us from having children. She cried a lot that day and even asked me to divorce her, but I did not take any of that to heart. It was no one's fault that we couldn't have children, but there were nights I thought of what it would be like to be a father, to have married a different woman – rather, one woman in particular.

Akanksha Devdhar and I had studied together in Xavier's College. We were in the science stream. She was good at maths and would often help me with it. We would meet after class and visit the art galleries that I liked and the kebab stalls which she enjoyed. We watched a few movies too.

I did not know what she thought of me, but I wanted to marry her. Of course, I never expressed my emotions – afraid she would reject me – and was content to enjoy her company as a friend. But things soon changed.

It dawned on me after the second year that science was not the right field for me. I was ignoring my painting, and if I went on like that, I would end up a clerk or something similar.

Akanksha tried to change my mind, but I was determined and took admission the next year in J.J. School of Arts. The journey thereafter was not smooth, but after a lot of hard knocks, I became a reasonably famous painter.

The best part of life at J.J. was meeting Shreya. I had specialized in painting while she was doing sculpture. Her sweet nature, and our interest in art, brought us together. We got married immediately after graduating.

I continued to meet Akanksha, but only for the first two years after joining J.J. It was clear she did not have Sumit the painter in mind. It was somebody else she wanted.

Thoughts of having a family with Akanksha left me feeling ashamed, guilty. I loved Shreya and felt like I had betrayed her.

One night, the silence was shattered by the ringing phone.

As I had presumed, it was Dr Shirali again.

'Please forgive me for disturbing you again,' the doctor pleaded. 'But do you know any Akanksha Devdhar?'

I sprang to my feet.

'Hello? Are you there?' the doctor asked.

'Yes … I do happen to know one Akanksha Devdhar. But what about her?'

'The boy says she's his mother.'

'What? Akanksha?'

'Yes, you heard that right,' the doctor said, sounding a little impatient. 'And that Sumit Sarang is his father.'

'I'll come to the clinic. Give me your address.'

The doctor was waiting at the reception.

'Extremely sorry to have you here at midnight. I don't normally stay this long at the clinic, but the case is … strange. Let me offer you some background before you meet him. Please, sit. Make yourself comfortable.'

I sat down and lit a cigarette.

'The boy was brought in an hour ago by a friend of mine who works for social services. The boy was seen roaming the streets in a confused state. My friend spoke to him and asked where he wanted to go. The boy asked him, "Are you a cop?" My friend was surprised to hear "cop" instead of "police officer". He said, "No, I'm just a friend. Where do you want to go?" The boy gave him an address which my friend could not understand. The boy took a diary out of his pocket and said he wanted to go there as his parents were waiting for him. He was in tears.'

'Did your friend take him there?'

'That was not possible. The address was of a suburb in Chicago, Naperville.'

'The child must have lost his mind.'

'My friend thought the same thing and brought him here, to a psychiatrist. I gave him some food and asked the usual questions. My friend left after dropping him off. The boy keeps insisting we take him to his parents. He's on the verge of a breakdown.'

I stubbed my cigarette and we went in.

The boy was chatting with the nurse when we entered. She was trying to get him to sleep. He stopped talking upon seeing me and then rushed over. He kept looking at me and said, 'Daddy, you look so different!'

'I'm not your daddy!' I was about to say, but I couldn't. He was such a cute boy: fair, with almost pink cheeks. Chubby too. If only he were my son. *Banish the thought!* I liked it when I heard the word 'daddy.' It felt good. No one had called me that ... before.

'My daddy is fatter than you but he looks like you,' he said, speaking in Marathi. 'He wears specs and his hair is grey. You take me home. You can see my daddy then.'

'Where do you live?'

'In America. But doctor uncle says this is India. It's quite far off, they say. How will I go home then?'

'Don't worry. We'll sort this out.' He seemed to trust me. I asked, 'You didn't tell me your name.'

'Sameer. But they call me Sam.'

His parents were Maharashtrians and he was fluent in both Marathi and English. But he had an American accent.

So his claim that he lived in America was not a sign of madness. But how did he get here?

'I'm confused,' he said, sitting close to me and resting his head on my shoulders. 'I had gone to school, and in my free period, I was walking in my school ground. There is a forest at the edge of it. Dense woods. I'm scared of the forest – it's so scary! I sat at the edge of the ground, looking at the sky above. I was watching two clouds floating in the sky and I must have fallen asleep. When I woke up, I was lying in a ground here. The sky was dark. It was night.' Sam started crying softly.

'Don't cry,' I said, ruffling his hair affectionately. He started sobbing harder. 'Don't cry. Everything is going to be okay.'

'He's a bright boy,' the doctor said. 'He told me his residence number when he came in. His parents must be worried sick. I dialled the number he gave me.'

'What happened?'

'Well, there was no ring. Nothing! No connection.'

Sam was sobbing softly.

'Give me the number,' I said, to console him. 'I'll try again when I get home.'

I took the number and noted the email address he gave me.

'Now, look here, Sam. The whole thing is very confusing, and we haven't got the slightest clue ... it is not possible to send you to America right away. But we will do the next best thing. Let's play a game. Let's pretend that you are a guest from America. I am your dad, isn't it? Then, let's go home. You'll meet your auntie there – someone like your mom. I'm sure you'll like her.'

It's so easy to convince a child. He stopped crying and was silent. Finally, he managed to smile.

I had the house key, but rang the bell. I wanted to wake Shreya.

She opened the door at the second ring. She must have presumed it was the milkman and was surprised to see me at the door. 'Where had you gone? And who is this?'

'He's Sam,' I said pushing him ahead. 'And she is Shreya auntie.'

'Hi.'

'He's my dad,' Sam said. Shreya looked at him, surprised. 'Dad?'

'I will explain everything later. Let him first eat something. And make some arrangement for him to sleep...'

Sam was not sleepy. He seemed dazed by the turn of events. He was not hungry and only had a glass of milk. 'I like milk,' he said, 'but my friends don't. I think it's just great!'

Shreya prepared a bed for him in the other bedroom. I lent him my t-shirt then put a blanket on him and switched on the fan. As I was switching off the light, I bid him goodnight.

'Goodnight, Shreya auntie,' he said, as he tried to sleep.

I had changed into my night clothes, but Shreya was in no mood to sleep. She said, putting her arms around me. 'Now, tell me: what is this all about?'

'Good night,' I said, trying to avoid her eyes. 'I will tell you in the morning.'

'Tell me now.'

'What do you want to know?'

'The boy – who is he? Why is he calling you dad?'

'That's because I resemble his dad.'

'What's his father's name?'

'Sumit Sarang.'

'That's you!'

'No. He is someone else. Sam told me while we were driving over. This Sumit is not a painter. He is a consultant with the Bank of America. He was born here and did his MSc in computer technology. He probably borrowed money from Akanksha Devdhar's father.'

'Wait a minute! Did you say Akanksha Devdhar?'

'That's what Sam said. She kept her maiden name.'

'Didn't you have a friend named Akanksha Devdhar? If I am not mistaken, she was with you in Xavier's College.'

'Yes.' I was hoping she would not discuss it further. 'There can be someone with a similar name.'

'But to have two such similar names ... isn't that too much of a coincidence? Tell me, with whom did he come from America?'

'No one.' I had lost my sleep now. 'That's the whole mystery. He says he dozed off in his school ground there and woke up here! We have to solve the mystery. We have to find a way to safely get him to his home.'

Shreya was not convinced. But I was happy that she was not jumping to conclusions about Sam being my illegitimate child. Finally, she dozed off.

Sleep eluded me. I could detect a pattern. Sumit Sarang was not a painter ... he did his MSc in computer technology ... went to America and married Akanksha. Sameer was born. My son with Akanksha ... was this really a pattern?

Sam slept until late the next morning. I could afford to defer my studio work but Shreya could not. Her exhibition of ceramics was four days away. She managed to reschedule a few appointments, delegate work and found time to speak about Sam.

'It was good that you brought him here,' Shreya said, talking of the previous night. 'But keeping him here is not solving the problem. We need to know who he is and where he is from.'

I tried the phone number once again, but there was no ring. No connection. I left a message on the email address, but suspected it would not reach the right person. I don't know why I felt so. Sam said his home was in Chicago? Why was the phone not getting connected? It was not possible that he would give a wrong number.

'I feel he is not alone. He came with someone and then was lost in a crowd. Who knows? The one who brought him here may have deliberately abandoned him.'

'Without any luggage? Without even a wallet?'

'He may have taken all that away. Could some criminal gang be behind all this?'

'Had that been the case, he would have mentioned it.'

'He might have been coached to say things.'

'It does not look like he is parroting anything. And he doesn't look scared. Had he been scared he would have confided in the doctor instead of mentioning my name.'

'Shall we inform the American Embassy? They could arrange to send him back.'

'Good suggestion, but he says I look like his dad and acts like he believes I *am* his father! How do we convince the embassy that we have nothing to do with this?'

'Frankly, we need to report it to the police. Or we may end up as suspects!'

'Hmm ... my worry is that they might put him in a mental hospital after listening to his story. The worst would be if he is sent to some orphanage.'

We thought of it for a long time but could not reach a conclusion. We had to do something fast lest our delay be misconstrued.

We decided not to go to a police station but to take the advice of Sabnis, a friend of mine, who was an assistant commissioner of police.

We woke Sam up at breakfast. He was confused for a while when he awoke. But he felt assured by my presence. He was willing to face the situation only because he was assured that I was with him. I was in my own world, imagining him to be my real son. The very thought was soothing. I had not experienced fatherhood, but thanks to this boy, I got close. It did not matter who he was. In my mind, I had accepted him as my son. My son ... with Akanksha!

Sam was hungry and he gobbled the sandwiches and eggs made by Shreya. He also liked the apple juice. We sat chatting as he ate. He spoke in a mature manner, for his age.

'Have you read the latest Harry Potter? *The Goblet of Fire*?' I asked.

'Harry Potter? Never heard of him. Who is he?'

I was surprised. How is it possible that children of his age in America do not know of Harry Potter? They are, in fact, crazy about the books.

'You are kidding!' I said. 'How come you don't know Harry Potter?'

But he really did not know. He loved to read and had read a lot from *Treasure Island* to *Parkinson's Laws*. As per him, Harry Potter had not come to America – maybe, it was published in the UK.

I was confused. He seemed a hundred per cent American, but in his America there was no Harry Potter.

Shreya listened to our chat and commented once in a while. I was getting more and more intrigued.

'You will see a lot of McDonald's here. You'll feel at home,' I said.

'McDonald's is okay,' he said. I breathed a sigh of relief. Thank god, he did not say there were no McDs in America. 'But McD is outdated there. The real thing is Bugs Bunny!'

He was talking about the latest chain of restaurants which had gathered popularity. He added, 'Mom says carrots are good for health.'

Sabnis visited us that afternoon. Shreya had called him up in the morning. I was planning to take Sam to his office, but he advised us against it to avoid unnecessary publicity. He came to our house in plain clothes instead.

He sat and spoke with Sam at length, talking about America and American cops. I did not interfere. I wanted Sabnis to come to his own conclusion. Shreya was out working.

After speaking with Sam, Sabnis called out to me. He said, 'Sumit, did you hear? He says he visited the World Trade Center last week. No, not the site – he was in the World Trade Center! As per him, 9/11 never happened. The towers are still there. When I told him about the attack, he merely said it sounded interesting, as if I were telling him a story. In his America, Bush was never elected president. He says Al Gore is a very popular president!'

'Sabnis, what exactly is going on?' I asked him, while Sam was reading a book.

'Well, it's good that I saw this for myself. Otherwise, I would not have believed you. It's not an ordinary event, so common sense or logic won't work here. We could assume he's been bluffing about being from the US, but he's a resident there, no doubt.'

'How is it that he has no knowledge of an event like 9/11?'

'That's because it did not happen in his America. He does not have Bush in his country. He has Al Gore. He has information, but it's different. Alternative.'

'I don't understand.'

'Imagine ... if Bush had lost the elections ... if the push against Laden had not been strong, and if the Twin Towers had not fallen. If Harry Potter had not reached America. It did not happen, but it could have happened. The possibility exists. There can be many such worlds. It's an alternate world. An alternate universe!'

'I can understand what you're saying. The thought did occur to me last night. But I'm not sure.'

'Think calmly. Our knowledge is limited. Our thoughts are restricted to the knowledge and information we have, but there are so many things in the world that cannot be explained. We need previous experience to measure such things. Anyway, the problem we have here is much more practical. We have to decide what to do with Sam.'

'I am fine to let him stay here. He calls me dad!'

'We have to follow some procedures. Our normal procedures are not of much use here. It is best to avoid getting stuck in the police bureaucracy. But we need to know how Sam arrived here. We must talk to Dr Shirali.'

'When you say procedures, are you talking of releasing an advertisement for his parents?'

'No. If you do that we might get a lot of people posing as his parents. Let his real parents file a complaint with the police regarding a missing child. I will leave instructions with my officers on what to do if we get such a complaint.'

The next day I took Sam to my studio. He was impressed with my paintings. 'This is fantastic! So far I have never seen a real painter.'

I gave him paints and a few sheets of drawing paper. He started painting: Bugs Bunny, a whale, tall buildings, aeroplanes.

Remembering something, I took out my old files, which had hundreds of newspaper cuttings, paintings and photos. I found the photo I was looking for. It was Akanksha, standing in a garden and smiling into the camera. I had taken the photo at a picnic. I had later made a portrait of it.

I said, giving it to Sam, 'Sam, who is this?'

'Anybody I know?' he asked.

'Sure. Doesn't she look like your mom?'

'A little ... but mom's a bit plump,' he said, studying the photo. 'But, yeah, my mom smiles just like this!'

Akanksha ... where is she these days? Is she in America? Is she desperately looking for Sam? How was I to inform her that he was okay?

I took Sam to the beach in the evening. I had decided to spend as much time as I could with him.

The crowds were thin and Sam enjoyed splashing around. He was constantly asking questions while I tried to answer them.

Finally, tired, we sat down. I perched on a rock while Sam sat in the sand, making sandcastles.

The sky was turning a lovely golden-yellow. Two solitary clouds moved slowly. I was dwelling over what Sabnis had said. His theory of alternate worlds. Many worlds of what ifs…

What if I had not gone to J.J.? I could have got my MSc.

What would have happened then? I would have finished my MSc. I surely would have married Akanksha. I would have gone to America, taking a loan from her father. I would have studied computer technology and made a career in banking or finance. Akanksha would have taken up a management job.

And then … Sameer would have been born. We would have called him Sam.

Akanksha may have put on a little weight, but her smile would not have changed. I too would look a little fatter. And would be wearing specs. My hair would have turned a little grey, thanks to the stress at work. All of that was possible – was a reality in a different universe.

Sam existed in that universe. Sam had moved miraculously from that reality into mine.

The sun had turned red. I said, as I watched it set, 'Come on, Sam! Let's go.'

But I did not receive a response. The sandcastle was there, but he was gone! I looked around, shouted his name. But he was nowhere to be seen.

I missed a heartbeat. *Where did go?*

I shouted out his name again.

There was silence all around me. I scanned the entire beach in the dying light of the sun. I checked the edge of the water, too. Sam was nowhere to be seen.

But my heart told me there was no point searching for him. Sam was not on the beach. He was not in this world. Not in *my* world. He had returned. Or, perhaps, he had gone to a different reality altogether.

A thought struck me then.

Did he really come here? Did he exist at all, or was it my imagination? Like the way I imagined getting married to Akanksha, becoming a father.

No, that was not possible. Others had seen him too. Dr Shirali, Shreya, Sabnis…

Regardless of what had been, he was gone now. The son that I had with Akanksha was gone.

I opened the door to find Shreya there.

'Shreya, Sam's gone,' I said.

'Gone? Where?'

'Wherever he came from. To his parents. To Akanksha.'

'But Akanksha…'

At that moment, a woman wearing a lovely Punjabi salwar-kameez walked in. She looked a little on the heavier side. She smiled. The same smile!

'Aaa … kank … sha!'

She laughed out loud saying, 'You look like you've seen a ghost. Didn't you recognize me in this?'

'I did, but how come you're here?'

'It's thanks to me,' Shreya said. 'I spent the entire afternoon searching for all Devdhars listed in the telephone directory. Finally, I found someone who knew Akanksha Devdhar. It was in fact she who picked up the phone at her father's place.'

'I came to Mumbai the day before yesterday.'

'From America?'

'Oh no!' Akanksha laughed once again. 'From Punjab. Randhir is an advocate in Hoshiarpur. He manages the family farms too. I've been in Punjab ever since I got married. But I do come here to meet Papa once in a while.'

'And your son...'

'I don't have one. I have a daughter.'

At that moment an eight- or nine-year-old girl came out and hugged Akanksha. 'This is Anushka,' Akanksha said. 'Beti, say hi to uncle!'

'Hello, uncle!' Anushka said shyly.

THE MAN ON THE BRIDGE

The moment Ranjit saw Dadaji for the first time, he formed a poor opinion of him. Dadaji was Ranjit's father's devoted servant. He had been in the service of Surjit Singh for the past twenty-five years, and had been with him until he breathed his last. Even in a remote place like Lohagadh, he stayed with Surjit Singh during his later years and ensured that he was well taken care of.

Ranjit knew all this, but was an odd person when it came to judging others. Just because Dadaji had grey eyes, it didn't make him shrewd, nor did being a man of few words make him suspicious – but it was difficult to explain this to Ranjit.

Dadaji was old but fit, and he worked tirelessly. He would pick up one task after another, even without being told. Ranjit found this very annoying. 'How much work could there be in a household of two people?' he'd ask. But, in a place like Lohagadh, you hardly found anyone to do tasks like grinding flour or cutting wood. That is why Dadaji had to plan all the chores in advance and do them a day earlier. As a matter of fact, one could say that work was an addiction for him.

Ranjit was the exact opposite. He was an only son and knew his father's wealth would soon be his. After all, the money from the iron business was enough to keep him comfortable without ever breaking a sweat. He strongly believed that if a young brat like him did not indulge in wine, women and other pleasures, who else would? He was also short-tempered and always ready for a quarrel – or a brawl. That attitude kept most people at bay.

Ranjit had done a lot of things in life. He had got a solid education, went on foreign trips, worked for a few years, ran businesses and incurred losses. Any money he did make, he was quick to spend. Once Surjit Singh grew old, he moved to Lohagadh – to his ancestral home. Ranjit continued to live in Delhi. He didn't marry but had multiple affairs. He managed to wriggle out of them unscathed. He made friends and a few enemies too. In short, he lived life on his own terms.

Suddenly, he got news of Surjit Singh's death. At that time, Ranjit was in Patiala on business. Dadaji had performed his employer's last rites. Ranjit was filled with regret the moment he got the news. But it is difficult to say whether the sorrow was for his father's death or that an outsider like Dadaji had performed his father's last rites.

The Lohagadh mansion fell vacant once Surjit Singh died. On a whim, Ranjit decided to go and stay in the village. There was little that Delhi had to offer him – no wife, no friends. He had spent so many years in the city, he figured it was time to enjoy the tranquillity of a village. He handed over his business to his partner, made arrangements for a steady income and headed straight for Lohagadh.

Lohagadh village seemed to be stuck in the past. There were a few settlements but more than half the village was now in ruins. From the collapsed structures, it was evident that it must have seen the heights of brilliance once upon a time. The dilapidated fort, the crumbling temples and mosques gave the place a dreary atmosphere.

Surjit Singh's mansion too had the same sullen air. It was a sprawling but lonely structure. At a little distance from the mansion was a lake of murky water. There were dense woods on the other side of the lake. In the darkness of the night, it was easy to imagine someone hiding in those woods. The lake was wide and a wooden bridge stretched over it.

Ranjit surveyed the mansion with Dadaji.

The architecture was a little confusing. Adjacent to the spacious drawing room was a narrow chamber. A very low door opened to stairs that led to another door, which opened into the veranda.

Ranjit said, smiling, 'Wah! A perfect spot to commit murder, isn't it?'

The way Dadaji threw a glance at Ranjit, his smile quickly vanished.

Ranjit continued, 'Do you know of any murder having taken place here?'

Dadaji shook his head absent-mindedly. Ranjit frowned as his joke had fallen on deaf ears. He did not like gloomy people.

With little to do, Ranjit took his time completing whatever task he was engaged in. He would sit in the sun for a long time just to dry his hair. He would smoke while taking in the view of the lake, play a game of patience, read novels, or recall old memories as he sipped his whiskey. At such times, he would wish Dadaji were a talkative character. But Dadaji would never even approach him unless called for. He would busy himself in some corner of the mansion, cleaning a lamp, removing cobwebs, or completing similar chores. Irritated, Ranjit would deliberately call for him and Dadaji would go to him at his usual slow pace.

'Where were you?' Ranjit would bark. 'My throat has turned dry shouting your name.'

Dadaji would stand there, without a word, and wait for instructions.

That would incense Ranjit further. 'Why are you standing here like a statue? Who is going to wash this tumbler? Your—'

Mindful of Dadaji's age, Ranjit would hold back the obscenities. 'Were you as reticent with Bappaji too?'

Dadaji would stare at Ranjit with his grey eyes for a moment and then pick up the tumbler. Ranjit would assume that his stare meant, '*Your Bappaji was different! Don't even compare yourself with him! Why should I bother to talk to you?*'

The very thought would make Ranjit boil with rage. He would mutter, caressing his long whiskers, 'I will put you in your place. Don't try to act smart!'

Ranjit sat in the balcony looking at the lake as he nursed a whiskey.

Suddenly, he detected movement on the bridge and stared at it intently. Ranjit had been watching the bridge for a long time and had not seen anyone in the woods behind the lake, or crossing the bridge.

It was a tall and well-built man in an overcoat. In the fading evening light, Ranjit could not see his face clearly. It looked as if his face didn't exist and was just a black hole.

The stranger was walking briskly towards the mansion after having appeared suddenly in the middle of the bridge. How was that possible? Ranjit was confused. Did he miss seeing the person step on to the bridge?

The silhouette grew larger and was getting clearer. Ranjit squinted but still couldn't see the face clearly. Finally, he turned and shouted for Dadaji.

Dadaji was busy cooking and it was only after Ranjit had shouted a few times that he realized that his employer was calling him. With age, his ability to hear and see had weakened considerably. He stood in front of Ranjit, wiping his hands with a cloth. Ranjit barked angrily, 'Can't you come when called the first time?'

Dadaji did not react.

'Anyway, who is that man? Do you know him?' Ranjit pointed in the direction of the bridge.

Dadaji narrowed his eyes and asked, 'Which man, sahib?'

Ranjit looked at the bridge. There was no one there!

'There was a man there. I saw him clearly. He was walking towards the mansion.'

Dadaji was quiet, making Ranjit angry.

'Do you think,' he burst out, 'I am imagining things? Am I hallucinating? Just because I had a little whiskey? I swear I saw that man walking towards the mansion.'

Dadaji stayed silent. Slapping the hand towel on his shoulders, he started climbing the steps.

'You remain quiet,' Ranjit continued his muttering, 'but I know people like you very well. Maybe you feel I disturb you and call you with some excuse or the other. Do you think it's my hobby?' He downed the remaining whiskey in one gulp and said, 'The man was walking towards the mansion. There is no doubt about it. I saw him clearly.'

Dadaji continued walking away, ignoring his rant. Ranjit presumed that the man must have gone down the bridge while he was talking to Dadaji and must have stopped somewhere near the mansion. *He may knock at the door any moment now!*

Ranjit listened in the silence of the night. He was listening for footsteps at the door.

But no one came. Ranjit started doubting himself now. The grave-like silence was a sharp contrast to the hustle and bustle of Delhi. Maybe he was subconsciously waiting for someone. But Dadaji's reaction, or rather lack of response, angered him. If only that fellow was willing to chat!

With each passing day, Ranjit found the mansion more and more depressing.

Another evening. There was no sound except for the birds chirping at the edge of the lake. Ranjit was flipping through an English novel and had finished his drink. Dadaji was busy preparing dinner.

When Ranjit glanced out of the window, he saw it again.

Someone stood at the edge of the bridge.

It was the stranger in the loose overcoat. He was facing the other side and started walking slowly towards the bridge.

Ranjit noticed he wasn't walking the way he had been the other day. He was holding a sack in his hand. It must have been heavy for he was struggling to drag it along.

Ranjit stared at the man. Why was that man dragging the sack towards the bridge?

At dusk, the silence was oppressive. Even the birds had stopped chirping. The man reached the middle of the bridge with the sack. Then something surprising happened.

He threw the sack into the lake.

Even though Ranjit was at a distance, it felt strange not to hear a splash. It seemed as if he were watching a silent film. Ranjit decided to run towards the bridge and see who that man was. He wanted to know what the man had carried in the sack. He put on his sandals quickly and stepped out of the mansion. He did not forget to pick up the large stick from near the door.

He rushed towards the bridge and was shocked at what he saw. Or what he didn't see.

There was no one on the bridge.

Unlike the last time, the stranger's disappearance could not be explained. He had been right in the middle of the bridge. Ranjit had rushed out the moment he had seen the sack drop. How could he vanish so soon?

A sudden thought entered Ranjit's mind. Had the man jumped into the lake after throwing the sack?

Ranjit reached the middle of the bridge and peered down.

The water was still. Not a wave or disturbance of any sort. The reflections of the tree branches over the water moved very slowly.

The birds started chirping once more. Even the crickets joined in.

Ranjit returned to the mansion, banging the stick on the ground in frustration. Suddenly a bandicoot, disturbed by the noise, rushed across the garden, screeching.

As soon as Ranjit stepped into the house he shouted, 'Dadaji! Dadaji…'

Dadaji was busy folding clothes. He came out carrying Ranjit's pyjamas and stood in the hall.

'Who is that man? Why does he come here repeatedly?' Ranjit shouted.

'Which man, sahib?' Dadaji asked calmly.

'The same man! The one I saw the other day. You thought I was hallucinating, but I saw him again. Just now – walking across the bridge. He threw a sack into the water. Yes, I saw it myself. With my own eyes! And my eyes are not weak like yours.'

'I did not see anyone,' Dadaji said and started walking away.

'Where are you going? I'm not done yet!' Ranjit shouted.

Dadaji turned and stood there obediently. Ranjit hated his silent obedience. It irritated him no end. 'What do you think? Who could it be? The way he disappeared suddenly … is it a man or a ghost?'

'I don't know, sahib,' Dadaji said.

'You know I don't believe in ghosts.'

Dadaji sat on the steps. Ranjit thought he smiled a little, but it was difficult to make out through his white moustache.

'I have seen a lot, but never a ghost. Arre, there are no ghosts! Let it come. I will squash it here itself!' Ranjit paused, hoping that Dadaji would comment. He let out a deep sigh. *Why does this man stay so quiet? Why does he not answer? Talking to him is like words bouncing off a wall.* Ranjit wanted him to argue, to insist that ghosts did exist.

Surely, in all those years, he would have seen something. Clearly, Dadaji would remain forever loyal to Bappaji. His son was not his responsibility, not someone he wanted to speak to.

Ranjit fumed and fretted. He felt lonely and it infuriated him that the bloody, silent fool would refuse to keep him company. In reality, had Dadaji told him ghost stories, Ranjit would have ridiculed him. But none of that happened and Ranjit was denied the satisfaction. Dadaji walked away silently when his employer stopped talking.

He turned at the door to look at his employer. Ranjit was muttering something to himself.

Ranjit could not sleep that night. He wondered why seeing the man on the bridge troubled him so much. He could not stop thinking about him. He ridiculed the very idea of ghosts, but how could he explain the disappearing man? It was as if he had witnessed something from the past.

The next morning, Ranjit went for a walk around the mansion. Dadaji gave him no information, but Ranjit was certain the apparition had something to do with his sprawling new home.

The houses closest to the mansion were further down the road. They belonged to labourers, who were often away working in nearby towns and villages. Ranjit managed to meet a few of the residents and introduced himself. They treated him with respect as he was Surjit Singh's son, and told him about the village, the crops they grew and even about the mansion.

No one mentioned ghosts, nor had anyone seen a person dragging a sack across the bridge.

There was more investigating to do.

It was night.

Ranjit poured himself yet another drink, unmindful of the late hour. He was taking to the bottle more frequently these days. His mind, tired of thinking about the event, needed the whiskey to calm it down.

Dadaji was busy chopping wood behind the mansion.

The *khut ... khut* of his chopping was disturbing Ranjit. It was otherwise silent and pitch dark outside.

Why the hell is he chopping wood? Maybe for the kitchen. He has been chopping for a long time. Why has he not finished yet? Why doesn't he sit with me here, in the balcony? Shall I call him? Shall I order him to chat with me?

Khut ... khut ... khach ... khach. Ranjit wondered why the old man was so stubborn and silent. And suspicious.

Khut ... khut ... khach ... khach...

It was entirely possible that Dadaji was keeping something from him.

Khut ... khut ... khach ... khach...

Stop that bloody noise! I know you are working. I know I sit here twiddling my thumbs, doing nothing! Yes, I know my father was a hard-working person and I'm feeding off his wealth...

The noise was becoming impossible to tolerate. Ranjit got up from his chair.

He staggered a little and realized he had a few more pegs in him than usual.

With some effort, he got to the rear of the mansion, where Dadaji sat chopping wood. Before Ranjit could speak, he froze in place. He saw a man running for his life.

Ranjit could not see his face but he seemed terrified and desperate to escape something.

Dadaji had stopped his chopping and was looking at him.

Within a moment, another man appeared from nowhere, chasing the man who had just run away.

Seeing his overcoat, Ranjit recognized him. It was the man on the bridge!

Again, Ranjit did not see his face, but he managed to spot the axe he carried. It glinted in the light of the lamp. Clearly, he was out to kill the other stranger, who finally stumbled and fell. Before he could get up, the axe met its mark. Repeatedly.

Blood sprayed and, suddenly, both of them disappeared.

Ranjit and Dadaji had just witnessed a heinous act.

Surprisingly, they had not heard a sound – no footsteps or screams – and there was no evidence of the murder left behind. It was as if nothing had happened. As if it had all been a dream.

But both of them were wide awake. Ranjit's mind was reeling under the effects of alcohol, but Dadaji was sober.

'Tell me,' Ranjit demanded, 'do you want to say nothing happened here? That you don't know anything?'

Dadaji was silent. He was too scared to speak.

'You rascal! This is what has happened in this mansion. Someone has been murdered and you know of it! You're hiding it!'

'No! I don't know,' Dadaji said, shaking his head vigorously.

'How can you say that? Speak! If Bappaji had a secret, I need to know. I'm his son! Tell me! Who is that man in the overcoat?'

Dadaji looked on with terror in his eyes and continued to shake his head.

Ranjit was furious. 'Tell me! Who is that man? Tell me!'

Dadaji continued to stare at him. He wanted to say something but words did not escape his lips. He was frozen with fear.

'You bloody rascal! Trying to hide from me, are you?'

A surge of rage flashed through Ranjit's mind. *The nerve of this servant! Trying to hide things from me! My father's secret ... Something needs to be done. I need to teach him a lesson for life.*

Before he could realize what he was doing, he picked up the axe and raised it, ready to swing.

Dadaji ran for his life. Ranjit chased him until Dadaji stumbled and fell.

Finally, Ranjit swung the axe – once, twice. Blood sprayed all over Ranjit before he came to his senses.

What had he done? He had murdered Bappaji's loyal servant. He had killed a poor man!

Why? What had he done to deserve it? Was this destined to happen? He looked around for a way to dispose of the body and spotted a sack of coal. He frantically emptied it, pushed in the corpse, and tied it with rope before dragging it to the bridge.

As soon as he reached the centre of the bridge, he threw the sack into the water.

Ranjit heaved a sigh of relief when it sank, but suddenly he felt strange. He had seen this before, but in reverse order.

Realizing who the man in the overcoat was, Ranjit gathered his housecoat and rushed back towards the mansion.

TWO KIDS

When the two kids arrived at the gate, the moon was hidden behind clouds. The poor children looked tired and their stomachs ached with hunger. They were famished.

They were young children: a girl of eight or nine years, and a boy of six. They both looked weak, but their faces were bright, in contrast to their scrawny bodies. Their cheeks were pink and full, and their eyes twinkled. Their hair had a pinkish tinge, but they had accumulated so much dust and grime that it was difficult to guess the original colour. Their complexion was pale and almost yellow, but their lips were a striking blood-red.

They were probably beggar kids. It was difficult to guess how they had such red lips and bright eyes. Their tattered clothes looked as if they had not been washed in a long time.

It was not clear where they had come from, but they were so tired that they stumbled as they walked. They were trying to keep each other motivated even though they had lost hope.

To add to their misery, it rained heavily. Before they could realize it, they were drenched. They decided to wait under the awning of a shop that had closed for the day, but it provided little protection against the strong wind. Every time the rain seemed to subside, they would try to step out – only for it to pour harder.

It was nearly midnight. The roads were empty and all doors and windows were shut. Even the street dogs were in hiding.

When the rain finally stopped, they walked on hand-in-hand. They knew that they had to ignore the hunger pangs and keep walking – if they hoped to find food.

They soldiered on, well into the less populated part of the town, where the houses were far apart. There were bungalows of different shapes and sizes, so different from the chaos of the chawls. Some bungalows looked occupied while others were empty and locked. A few had sloping roofs. In some, a light burnt in the veranda, while others were cloaked in darkness. All around them the wind whistled through the trees.

There was no one on the road except the two children. The dim, yellow light from the street lamps made the darkness seem more intense.

The children could not immediately decide on a house to approach in their search for food, but they walked on – towards the house at the end of the lane.

It was a single-storeyed house, but it had a small staircase, next to which a lamp burnt steadily in the dark. It looked as if the house was ready to devour an unexpected visitor.

The children stood at the gate as the moon hid behind the clouds.

It was darkness once more. The lamp at the bottom of the stairs looked lonelier than before. The children stared but could not see anything through the window of the room upstairs.

They grabbed on to the iron bars of the gate, which was enough to make it swing open with a loud screech. They wondered if anyone else had heard it.

Someone had. Suddenly, a man appeared at the window.

'Who is it?' he asked.

The children stood silently.

He repeated his question, 'Who is it?'

The children did not answer. All that came out of their mouths were faint groans.

The moon emerged from behind the clouds, casting its light on the children. The man downed his remaining whiskey, picked up the torch and walked down the stairs. He got to the gate and stood before the children, who seemed frightened by his huge body, dark colour and upturned moustache.

'Don't be afraid,' he said, smiling.

'Can we come in?' the boy asked.

'Yes.' He nodded.

'We're very hungry,' the boy said. The girl squeezed his hand.

'Come. Come upstairs, I will give you some food.'

The children followed him in through the main door. Even in the gloom of the drawing room they could see chandeliers and other expensive items.

The boy walked behind the man but the girl stopped at the door. 'Muddy feet…' she mumbled.

'Don't worry. My servant will clean it tomorrow. You come in!' the man said.

She entered and followed them as they made their way up the stairs, guided by torchlight.

There, the man pointed to a wooden door and said, 'There's the bathroom. You can wash your hands and feet.'

Obediently they stepped in and scrubbed themselves clean.

The man and his servant were the only occupants. There were no children in the house. The man took out two shirts and two white shorts. He waited at the table for the children to come out of the bathroom.

A lamp burnt over the table. The room had a bed and three chairs, along with a number of odd items. The single lamp was insufficient there, no match for the shadows that danced around it.

When the children came out of the bathroom, he took out a large towel from the armoire and said, 'Here. Wipe yourselves dry.'

The children stripped off their tattered clothes without hesitation, as if they had been waiting to be rid of them. The man picked up his glass of whiskey and sipped quietly as they stepped into the fresh set of clothes he pointed at. He looked at them as he sipped his whiskey wondering: *Who are these kids? Where have they come from?*

Many questions flooded his mind, but he did not feel like asking any. The whiskey had given him a pleasant buzz, which he did not intend to shatter.

The children, having changed into fresh, dry clothes, sat on the wooden chairs. They looked far better now. Pleasant and clean.

The utensils on the table suggested that the man had been having his dinner when they arrived at the gate. He set plates for them with bread and mutton curry. They pounced at the food while the man poured them some water before returning to his drink.

The children ate with a passion, slurping their food and licking their fingers. He asked, as he watched them eat, 'Where have you come from?'

They did not respond for a moment. The girl answered, licking her lips noisily, 'We are homeless.'

'I don't understand.'

'We stay on the footpath.'

A few minutes passed. The only sound in the room, apart from their slurping, was that of the clock on the wall ticking noisily.

'What about your parents?' he asked.

'We are orphans. We don't have anyone,' they answered in unison.

They have no one. No family and no home. His mind, numbed with alcohol, processed the information at its own pace. *Helpless and starving ... How do they survive?* He wondered how long it had been since their last meal.

He served them a few more slices of bread along with another helping of mutton curry before refiling his glass.

The children looked at him while they ate. He seemed good and kind – unlike so many who had turned them away. They wondered if it was all because he had no children of his own.

'You sleep here. Go tomorrow morning,' he said once they finished eating. There was no trace of emotion on his face when he said it.

He then spread a dhurrie on the floor and lay a sheet over it. 'Sleep,' he said.

The children lay down without a word and fell asleep with their arms around each other.

He sat there for a long time listening to the rain. The moon peeped out from behind the clouds and the road, visible from window, shone in the moonlight.

He finally stood up, glanced at the children once and then walked down the stairs to the drawing room, where his servant slept.

He said, waking him up rudely, 'Get up! Bring out the knives. There are children here – two of them!'

The servant got busy while the man returned to his chair upstairs.

The children slept fitfully.

The servant got to his feet as soon as he was ordered to. In the middle of the night, he was most often woken with the phrase 'There are children here.'

It was not that his master enjoyed waking him up at odd hours, but such was the nature of the trade. After all, one did not encounter small, unattended children very often. He had to make do with whatever he got, whether they were children kidnapped from villages, or those lost at the railway station. The bungalow was not on the main road. It was in one corner of the town. One needed time to drop the children here. And then, the task was best carried out in the middle of the night.

The servant had to be alert. He would have to carry out the task, even with the fear of the noose ending up around his neck. That was why he could not help but ask questions: *Where did the children come from? Were they sent by the regular man or did they come from some other source? Do they have parents? Would someone recognize them? Would there be a police complaint registered for missing children? Would the police be searching for them?*

Most of the children never had anyone important looking for them because they were from slums. How were their poor parents to register a complaint with the police? His employer was careful to pick children from underprivileged families or, better yet, orphans. He would not take unnecessary risks and made sure they could not be identified. To ensure that, he would have them disfigured. As a result, some had an eye removed while others had their lips torn open. The man who bought them even preferred the ones who looked pitiful and hideous – after all, they made better beggars. The man, who controlled a gang of beggar children, believed people often gave money out of fear. Horrible faces scared them and money could make the children leave them alone.

The job didn't bother the servant. He only did what the master told him to – and he was quick. His speed and precision could put a surgeon to shame. Doing it slowly would only be torture, and that was why he kept his instruments sharp and clean. They could not afford the hassle of infected wounds. He was efficient, and so his master treated him well. Like an equal.

The man, back in his chair, waited for the servant to finish preparing his tools. It wouldn't be difficult to answer his questions about the new children, who were different from the usual victims brought in by a middleman – who would have to be paid. This time, he had only the rains to thank.

How fortunate that simple inclement weather had brought two children to their gate. Two homeless orphans who looked pathetic enough to bring in good money. The buyer would love them, especially once they had them permanently disfigured.

The man got up from his chair and called for the servant in a low voice. He offered him a peg and then approached the children and woke them up.

The children got up immediately. For a moment, they were shocked to see the huge, dark frame of the servant. When the man said, 'Come,' they looked at each other for a moment and then followed him down to the drawing room.

It was dark and they walked further down, into a basement. The children were confused but continued to walk, stumbling and holding hands.

They held the bannister for support and finally they could feel the hard floor. The servant went ahead and pressed a switch. A dull, yellow bulb glowed.

The room was bare, except for a small table in the corner. It looked like a hospital bed, with frames on sides. A tray kept on its side had syringes in it. Next to it, on a small tray, were shining, sharp instruments.

The man was lost in thought. He was still drunk. The two children were a bonanza. He had used the profits from his trade to open a hotel and a liquor shop. He had made lot of money providing a small room next to the liquor shop for people to drink in. This was his side business. Earlier he would supply children and earn a commission. He later realized that if he provided 'ready' kids, those who were disfigured or had their limbs broken, he could earn a much higher commission.

He was wrenched out of his thoughts by a scream.

He downed the whiskey and went to the basement. It was silent. He assumed the children were unconscious and the servant was cleaning his instruments.

Poor kids! They had the misfortune of landing up here and ... For a moment, a pang of sympathy troubled him. A sure sign that he was drunk, he thought.

The sight that greeted him when he stepped into the basement made his blood run cold.

The children were nowhere to be seen. All that lay on the floor was the servant's dead body.

A bite wound on his throat spewed blood.

The children had to be close by, the man thought, gripped by fear. He rushed up the steps and got to the telephone. He somehow managed to dial the police station. 'Hello, hello! My servant ... he is dead. Someone slit his throat!'

'Hello! Who is speaking?'

He could not answer. The phone fell out of his trembling hand. What he saw terrified him.

The two children stood near him but they were completely transformed now. Their bodies were greenish, furry and beastlike. Their nails extended into claws. Their eyes remained unchanged – even as they shone like those of wolves – and their red lips were even brighter, slick with blood.

He tried evading them, but in an instant they were at his throat, sinking their fangs in as he collapsed.

The police inspector put the phone down reluctantly. He had not got an answer to the question he had asked. There was no way for him to know where the call had come from. The words rang in his mind...

'My servant ... he is dead ... someone slit his throat!'

The inspector wondered what he could do. There was no one to discuss the matter with. A lone havildar dozed outside.

'Someone slit his throat...'

The rain, which had stopped for a while, picked up again. The moon was behind the clouds now. It was darker than before.

The inspector sat thinking for a long time before busying himself with paperwork.

He suddenly remembered a circular that had been sent out a few days back:

> *Recently, a number of people have been found dead with their throats slit. No other clues have been found as of yet, and locals have been spreading rumours of shape-shifting ghosts. Please report any unusual activity.*

'Bullshit! Spirits and ghosts, my foot!' the inspector mumbled to himself. 'But I need to report today's murder.'

A shiver ran down his spine, but he didn't know why he felt uneasy. It was not the first time that he was alone at the police station at night.

Suddenly he raised his head and saw two children standing at the door.

Their tattered clothes were soaked and their pathetic faces made them look helpless. Yet, their eyes were surprisingly bright and their lips were red.

Poor kids! Drenched and helpless, the inspector thought.

'Can we come in?' they asked.

THE HANGMAN'S NOOSE

Shantaram was surprised to see Natha, a.k.a. Professor Ramnath Shaligram, arrive without any prior notice.

Natha, Shantaram and Vartak, had been friends since college. Vartak was never referred to by his first name, while Natha, despite being a professor of logic, remained Natha for them.

The gang had enjoyed college life together – throwing paper darts at other students, studying together and having chai in the canteen. Their paths diverged over the last fifteen or twenty years. Their letters had changed too – becoming dry and to the point, and often seeking specific favours. For example, Vartak would write to Natha if he had to recommend someone for a college admission, while Natha would write to Shantaram if someone he knew was passing by Shantaram's town and wanted to stay over for a night.

Their respective jobs had taken them to different towns. Shantaram was a bank manager while Vartak worked in the government treasury department and would get posted to small towns and villages.

Natha was a professor in a district college, teaching logic, reasoning and related subjects. His writings on topics such as conscience, life after death and current affairs had made him a local celebrity.

The three would reminisce about their college days, talking about them with their families. A chance meeting in a train or a bus would evoke memories and they would enjoy a cup of tea together. Their bond had remained strong, even if they didn't have as much time for each other as they once did.

Natha's sudden arrival was a pleasant surprise for Shantaram. Seeing that he wasn't carrying any luggage, he assumed Natha was staying at a hotel. But the muffler around his neck told him that he had just disembarked from a bus or a train.

Natha refused Shantaram's offer of food. Not that Shantaram could have offered him much, what with his wife being away at her mother's.

'You're staying for the night, aren't you? I'll make arrangements,' said Shantaram.

'No. I'll go back in a while.'

'What? At this hour?' Shantaram asked, a little surprised.

'I have to,' Natha said. 'I'm here to say something...'

Shantaram knew how obstinate Natha could be.

'Okay. Tell me what you have to say. Hope you're not in any kind of trouble.'

'I got a letter from Vartak some days ago. Just out of the blue. I'd written a story for a magazine. It explained that ghosts did not exist. He wanted to discuss that story.

'He said I lacked first-hand experience, and that he could show me ghosts in many parts of the village he's staying in.'

This had been the topic of discussion over many cups of tea in our college canteen. Natha would explain why he believed ghosts did not and could not exist, while Vartak would find reasons to tease him and deliberately oppose his argument. Shantaram observed Natha as he spoke animatedly, gesticulating in the air as he talked about Vartak's letter. He was a short, stout man, his dark face accentuated his bulging eyes, over which he wore thick glasses. He had a habit of removing his glasses while speaking before putting them on again. He had always been a little eccentric.

'I decided to accept Vartak's challenge,' Natha said, as he removed his spectacles while adjusting the muffler around his neck. 'I replied to his letter, stating the date of my arrival at his village.'

The town clock struck twelve as Natha continued his story. Except for the howl of a street dog, there was complete silence outside. Even the crickets seemed to have stopped chirping. The calendar on the wall flapped once as a breeze found its way through the open window. The lantern threw strange shadows on the wall as Natha continued his story.

'Vartak had promised to pick me up from the railway station,' Natha said, as he put his spectacles back on.

The train arrived nearly forty-five minutes ahead of schedule.

Natha stepped out on to the small and desolate platform. It was a very small village and he was the only passenger who got off. There was no one on the platform. Putting his bag down, he wiped his face and neck with his handkerchief. It was a humid night.

The train moved with a jerk. It had stopped for barely a minute. For a brief, tantalizing moment, Natha was tempted to jump back into the safety of the train. But soon enough, it had chugged its way noisily out of the station.

Natha looked around. He couldn't even spot a ticket checker. A mangy street dog lay on a solitary bench. What if he were to get mugged here? There was no one in sight! Natha wondered where Vartak was. But he had arrived nearly an hour in advance. It was difficult to wait for him in the dead of the night, in the darkness of the platform, all alone. Natha decided to walk to Vartak's house. After all, he had sent detailed directions in his letter.

As he stepped out of the platform, Natha realized there was neither a tonga nor a rickshaw-wallah to help him. He would have to walk. The directions were quite simple: he was to go straight until he reached a peepal tree surrounded by a cement platform. He had to turn right at the peepal tree and Vartak's bungalow would be another five minutes away. It was something he could not miss, Vartak had assured him.

Natha turned at the peepal tree as suggested, but the bungalow was nowhere in sight. He must have walked for nearly fifteen minutes. Who could he ask? There was no one in sight. To make thing worse, all the houses around were enveloped in deep silence.

Natha decided to retrace his steps and returned to the peepal tree. Maybe, he had walked farther than required. The peepal leaves rustled in the wind. Natha looked up and smiled at the night sky; it was glittering with stars. It was a new moon night – he remembered someone in the train mentioning it.

He said, laughing to himself, 'Why is a professor of logic, who does not believe in ghosts, thinking of a new moon under a peepal tree? These are things illiterate villagers talk about!'

He looked at his watch. It was twenty minutes to midnight.

He had been out for nearly an hour. Didn't Vartak say his house was just five or seven minutes from the railway station?

Natha decided to walk the other way. Maybe he had misunderstood the directions. He was forced to stop after walking for nearly fifteen minutes. The road vanished into a densely wooded area.

Natha wondered what he should do next. He cursed himself for having been impatient. He should have waited at the platform.

The sound of the crickets. Leaves rustled.

Natha glanced at his watch. It was midnight.

That was when he saw a lamp burning amidst the trees. He wondered how he had missed it.

He walked briskly towards the lamp, relieved that someone was up.

The house stood in the middle of a clearing. It was small and had little stepping stones leading to the door through the slushy mud. He gingerly stepped on one and then another. The place looked old, dilapidated.

Natha stood at the door for a few moments. There was no sound from within, but the burning lamp gave him enough confidence to knock. He waited for a while and then knocked again, this time a little louder. He heard someone shout, 'Coming.' Not seeing any movement, Natha was about to knock once more, when it opened.

At the door stood an emaciated man. His cheeks looked almost hollow and his eyes were sunken.

He was a sign of hope for Natha. The man said, 'Please, come in. I need some help.'

Natha was surprised. The man had not even bothered to ask for his name. Yet, Natha walked in without further questions.

They entered a dimly lit room where a lantern burnt in a corner. What he saw next froze him in place. In the middle of the room hung a hangman's noose. The rope swayed a little as a breeze entered the room. All Natha could do was stare at it unblinkingly.

He was almost hypnotized by the sight of it. It was as if he had been drugged. The dark, musty room ... the mildly swinging rope with the loop and knot ... the darkness outside ... it was all too much for him.

The old man stood near the noose. Natha had barely recovered from his initial shock when the man said, 'I was about to hang myself to death, you know.' His voice sounded as if he were speaking from inside a deep, narrow well. It did not suit his nearly skeletal body. 'But I couldn't tighten the noose. I need someone to help me. I will push the stool away and then ... this noose will tighten itself around my neck ... I will be free of my troubles. Forever! But I need help. I cannot do it alone. I need your help.'

The hollow voice mesmerized Natha. All he could hear was, 'I need your help. Your help.' He stood there dumbfounded, mechanically wiping the sweat off his neck and face, his eyes fixed on the noose.

He finally managed to find his voice and asked, 'But why end your life?'

'This disease...' the thin man replied. 'It's ruined my body. It won't go and it won't let me go! There is no happiness, only pain. Death is my only escape.'

His ardent plea tugged at Natha's heart. He realized that death was the only solution for this man. He could not bear to see his pain. He was being drawn to this stranger without completely realizing that he was about to help him die.

He touched the noose and finally found the nerve to put it around the man's neck, which felt more like a thin strip of bone.

'Thank you!' the man muttered. Natha tightened the noose.

The man stepped off and began swinging from the noose, but his feet still sought out the stool.

Natha kicked the stool away. Finally, the body went limp. Natha could not help but stare at the body of the man he had helped commit suicide.

He heaved a sigh of relief at the man's escape from pain. The soul had finally been set free, and he had helped.

He absently touched his own neck as if to reassure himself that he was still alive. He wondered if what he had done was wrong. He once again touched his neck. It was becoming a habit.

Vartak found Natha in a state of shock before he slumped on to the ground, his hand at his neck.

Vartak had looked around the station. There was no one there. He had waited at the platform for an hour, returning the next morning to wait for another train. Thinking that perhaps Natha had chickened out of the challenge, he went back, taking the route past the 'hangman's noose' corner. That's where he found Natha.

'Natha, Natha!' Vartak had to shake him back to his senses. Finally, after a while, he stirred and looked around, unable to understand how he had landed in that house.

'What are you doing here?' Vartak asked. 'Pick up your bag. Now.'

It was a bright and sunny morning. Natha looked around trying to recall how he had arrived there. He said, 'I ... I helped him...'

Vartak knew what he was trying to say. He said, 'Don't worry about it. You just fell victim to the new moon night. The man you're talking about killed himself years ago. Seems he still wanted to live, after all. This happens every new moon night. He lights a lamp and hangs himself by the rope. He finds an unsuspecting stranger like you to help him. That's why we call this place the hangman's noose.

Natha's mind barely registered what Vartak had said. He was in his own world, silent and brooding, much to Vartak's surprise. He had expected a heated argument about ghosts.

'It's not that I didn't understand what Vartak said,' Natha clarified. 'But that experience felt real to me. It's changed me, how I think and act. I tied my daughter's skipping rope into a noose one day, I don't know why.

'I can't stop thinking about it. Vartak keeps insisting that none of it was real, but that doesn't help. It was real enough to me. Real enough to have done something to my mind. One day, I tied my daughter's skipping rope into a noose. And when I'm drawing water from the well, I'm tempted to do the same, so I let the bucket fall only to feel it stop – hanging midway like a body. Like his body, in that small house.'

The doorbell rang, piercing the silence of the night.

Shantaram sprang to his feet. 'Who could it be at this hour?' he asked.

He opened the door to find a postman with an urgent telegram. Shantaram tore it open. He read it and screamed.

'No! It's not true. It can't be!'

'It is true, Shantaram,' Natha said, his voice steady.

'I need proof!'

Natha removed the muffler from around his neck.

He let Shantaram see the dark, red-black mark. The mark left by the rope from the well.

ABOUT THE AUTHOR

Ratnakar Matkari (born 1938) is a Marathi writer, a movie and play producer-director, and a self-taught artist. He worked as a columnist for newspapers and magazines in the 1970s. Matkari's works thus far include a number of plays, collections of one-act plays, books of his short stories, novels, and poems and plays for children. He has received twenty-one awards from different institutions including the Akhil Bharatiya Marathi Natya Parishad, the Maharashtra State Government, and the Sangeet Natak Akademi.

Vikrant Pande started translating from the Marathi with Ranjit Desai's classic novel *Raja Ravi Varma*, the story of India's most celebrated painter. He has since translated Milind Bokil's *Shala*, N.S. Inamdar's *Rau: The Great Love Story of Bajirao Mastani* and *Shahenshah: The Life of Aurangzeb*, Ranjit Desai's *Shivaji: The Great Maratha* and *Karna: The Great Warrior*. He is currently a vice chancellor with TeamLease Skills University, Vadodara.